A PLACE
OF SAFETY

A PLACE
OF SAFETY

Angela Burdick

SECKER & WARBURG
LONDON

First published in England 1988 by
Martin Secker & Warburg Limited
Michelin House, 81 Fulham Road
London, SW3 6RB

Copyright © 1988 Angela Burdick

British Library Cataloguing in Publication Data

Burdick, Angela
  A place of safety.
  I. Title
  823'.914[F]   PR6052.U6/

  ISBN 0 436 07589 X

Set in 10½/14pt Linotron Palatino by Deltatype, Ellesmere Port
Printed and bound in Great Britain by
Billing & Sons Ltd, Worcester

For M.

I caught this morning morning's minion, king-
   dom of daylight's dauphin, dapple-dawn-drawn Falcon, in his riding
   Of the rolling level underneath him steady air, and striding
High there, how he rung upon the rein of a wimpling wing
In his ecstasy! then off, off forth on swing,
   As a skate's heel sweeps smooth on a bow-bend: the hurl and gliding
   Rebuffed the big wind. My heart in hiding
Stirred for a bird, – the achieve of, the mastery of the thing!

Gerard Manley Hopkins, *The Windhover*

PART ONE

1

ONE PINT, SIX eggs, half a pound of butter, and Martha were delivered by the milkman one fine morning. When Edith went to fetch in the milk from the doorstep there was Martha, wrapped in a shawl and wearing a pink, silk, lace-frilled cap, curled up in a shopping-basket. She lay open-eyed, wise and quiet; 'civilized', as Edith told her Arnold.

Edith wasn't wise. She wasn't stupid, though; after all she had acquitted herself rather well at university, gaining a good Second and a reputation as something of an original. The parish magazine would collapse without her, and she rather fancied herself as a bit of a writer. Or rather hack, she would say with a deprecating smile. Arnold, the Rev. Arnold Mellors, was a man of the cloth.

Because he was so holy, she could never, you know, bring herself to do anything grubby with Arnold. Edith had never seen her own body naked, never looked at it in the mirror, never paused to admire her soft fair-haired skin. Neither had Arnold.

As night crept towards the burgeoning dawn, Edith scrubbed her face with cold water. Yesterday's milk made

3

tiny globs on the top of the tea she took to Arnold. She didn't recognize his smile of distaste as he sipped. He's happy, she thought. Such a lovely week, Easter week. The busiest week in the church calendar; so many people to meet, all the colour and splendour of the ritual to enjoy.

Edith went downstairs. It was still quite dark outside but she drew back the kitchen curtains anyway. Busy, busy she was, as she scurried around, washing and wiping. She tucked the teaspoons carefully into each other and worried the formica till it shone.

A large black cat unfurled itself slowly and stretched. Edith had laid the table for two. Blue and white egg cups set neatly down drew a sigh of regret, as she fancied herself fussing over unpossessed children, getting them ready for school.

She would tuck their scarves cosily around them, she thought, and caress their soft wee cheeks. The cat nudged its way past her as she walked towards the door. Yes, she would enjoy waving goodbye as they set off with little satchels strapped tightly to their backs, bright-eyed and smiling. The cat circled her legs impatiently.

'Puss, puss.' She pushed him away as he nudged her moving legs towards the front door. 'Time for your milkies.' She opened the door and bent down to pick up his morning milk. A pair of lapis-blue unfocused eyes stared at something above her head.

Edith had heard of babies being found on doorsteps, but, just for a moment or two, she thought perhaps this one was a very special delivery from Above; an answer to her prayer.

Nancy couldn't look at Harry. She woke late this morning, though for an hour she'd had a strange feeling something was wrong. The baby wasn't crying for her early bottle.

Harry had already returned from his milk round. She wrapped her gown about her and peered into the cot. The other children have gone to school without disturbing her, and how kind, she thought, Harry has taken the baby downstairs and fed her, so as not to wake Nancy. Perhaps he had taken to her after all.

She sat hunched up at the kitchen table, staring down at the frayed buttonhole of her gown. Slowly, and in a very low voice, she said:

'Where's baby?'

'Let me get you a cup of tea.' Harry set one down before her. 'Come on, drink up.'

'Where's baby?'

'Don't fuss. Everything is okay. Everything's for the best.' He nodded to himself. 'It's not everyone has the opportunity to have their problems solved for them. You should be thankful, you should.'

'Where's baby?'

'We won't have to be reminded any more of your sordid mistake, filthy bastard.' He was leaning towards her, hands pressing the table. 'Oh yes, you should be very thankful, very thankful indeed.' He stepped back. 'Drink your tea.'

'Where's my baby?'

'Your baby. That's right, it's your baby, your baby, your baby. Not mine. Dirty slut.' He stood up and slammed the chair back under the table.

'*Where is my baby?*' she screamed, tears running down her face, her nose dripping; a long, terrible, agonized animal noise came from somewhere inside her.

By the end of the week the children were whining and dirty, and Harry made himself pretty scarce. Molly Larkin, the next door neighbour, missed seeing Nancy and the little one, and noticed the state of the children. But when Nancy dropped the glass of water she handed to her, Molly Larkin knew it was serious. She saw to it that Nancy had her things with her, and handed in her bag when she saw her off in the ambulance.

'Bubb-bubb-bubb-bubby,' Nancy babbled incoherently. They took her away. They put her in a cubicle and never turned the light off. All night. They were very kind when they asked questions.

'Where is your baby?' they said and looked knowingly at each other when she replied: 'I don't know.'

'Where is your baby?'

'I don't know.'

'What have you taken?'

'Mogadon.'

'How many?' The doctor in his white coat tapped his pencil impatiently.

'Three or four a day since Tuesday, I think,' said Nancy.

'Breakfast, dinner and tea,' said the doctor.

But she couldn't really remember. They kept falling through her fingers. It seemed ridiculous that she couldn't do a simple thing like counting.

The curtains of the cubicle swished open. A great black eagle pushed past the doctor and flapped towards Nancy, tossing red flowers all over her. Harry, black coat flying open, sweaty and drunk again of course, said: 'I've risked my freedom for you.' He hovered, adjusting the flowers along the whole length of her body. They were red geraniums. 'The shops were shut so I pinched all the flowers from outside the Town Hall. I nearly got nicked by two policemen. I gave them a flower each and ran.'

'I should like to speak to you outside.' The doctor ushered Harry back out through the curtains.

In the morning they washed her face and tried to comb

6

her hair; but it was impossibly matted. They took her gently into another ward. She liked the feel of the fresh sheets and plumped-up pillows.

'Pleased to meet you,' said an imperious voice from the opposite bed. 'I do think you could have told me you were coming, though.'

Nancy was silent.

'Don't think you fool me, pretending to be asleep,' said the voice. 'Introduce yourself, please. I'm Mrs Appleby.'

'My name's Nancy Eagan,' mumbled Nancy.

'Mrs Appleby doesn't usually see visitors without an appointment,' said Mrs Appleby. 'In fact, Nancy, Mrs Appleby doesn't like to entertain at this hour of the day. Far too early,' Mrs Appleby offered. 'I was going to put my face on, but' – she patted the side of her head – 'you've seen me now, so I suppose there's not much point,' she sighed.

The door opened and a trolley clattered in, followed by a nurse, who brought them breakfast with a bright smile.

'The staff are frightfully good,' said Mrs Appleby to no one in particular. 'So difficult to keep them these days, of course.' She sighed again as she tucked into breakfast, carefully wiping her mouth between each forkful. When she finished she leant back against the propped-up pillow and closed her eyes.

Nancy took a comb and mirror from her bag, which appeared on the bedside table. She couldn't remember bringing it. She began to comb her hair. There was a matted clump at the back. How long was it? Three? Four days? She must have tossed and turned to get it in this state. She picked up the mirror, and stared at the unfamiliar face in surprise. There were bruises on her face, and a nasty graze that seemed painted onto her forehead, nose, and chin. She must have fallen, but she couldn't remember.

'You've changed the curtains,' exploded Mrs Appleby.

7

'How dare you!' She had Nancy in her sights. She fired. 'You've moved all the furniture. You have no right to invade my house, no right at all. Oh!' She let out an enormous sigh. 'This is so vexing.' She looked around the room abruptly, examining each corner in her survey. 'What have you done with my piano? Where is it? Mother left it to me. My beautiful piano,' she whined in her Best-Little-Girl-Voice. 'Dear Mother. What would she say to common people coming into my gorgeous house and changing everything around? Oh dear!' Another sigh. 'Mother would be so sad she isn't here to protect her darling Elizabeth, her baby Betsy, little Lizzie, beautiful Beth.'

'Excuse me . . .' – Nancy tried to sound prim – 'but I haven't done . . .'

'Don't interrupt!' Imperious again, Mrs Appleby lined up another volley. 'You have even changed the wall-paper. Without my permission. You are very wicked, wicked, wicked.'

Edith stood with one bottle of milk tucked inside her elbow and, nearly tripping, stepped backwards into the house. She didn't take her eyes off the baby until she snapped the door shut. She opened the door again and peered down for a better look. The baby was still there.

She shut the door, walked back to the kitchen, put some milk into a saucer, and placed it on the floor for the cat. It couldn't be true – her imagination was running away with her. Sometimes she felt faint when she got up quickly after bending down. Perhaps she was seeing things now. All those longings were making a mockery of her; she must remember to pay the doctor a visit. This was that time of life. After all, look what happened to poor Elizabeth Appleby with her strange imaginings. Just one more look, perhaps, to be quite sure.

Edith brought the basket up to her bed nervously; she was afraid she might somehow unintentionally drop the baby. She turned Martha out of the shopping basket and eased her onto the bed as if she were unpotting a plant. She turned her over. The baby was making urgent sucking movements with its mouth. She must fetch Arnold and get his advice, but she didn't know if the baby would roll off the bed.

She went to the open door and called him, turning back quickly to check that the baby was still where she had left it.

Arnold stood in his old grey dressing-gown and stared uncomprehendingly at Edith holding the baby in her arms and looking up at him.

'Edith! What have you done?' A Madonna picture flittered across his mind. He pushed it away. The word 'Virgin' replaced it, and then, 'Immaculate Conception', the bit the Catholics were so keen on. He was already in his pulpit stammering an embarrassed explanation.

'A little girl, dear,' said Edith, having had a quick look.

'Edith, whose baby is it?' Not Another Man, he thought, after all these years.

'I don't know, dear,' said Edith, placing a finger into the baby's hand.

Arnold leant against the door frame. She didn't even know for sure. Who would have suspected? Arnold slid slowly down the door frame. Edith, with a secret life and *more than one lover*! Arnold felt a soft grey velvet cloth envelop him.

'Arnold, wake up, wake up.' Edith roughly tapped the side of his face. Perhaps she should use mouth-to-mouth resuscitation, she thought. But that was only for drowning people, not fainting ones, and in any case Arnold might misinterpret her intentions when he came to.

9

2

HARRY WAS DISTRESSED when he came home. It wasn't just Nancy. He complained to Molly, who was minding his children, about losing the pocket-watch his grandfather had left him, and he was certainly the worse for drink. He insisted that Molly return home next door even as he paced anxiously about the tiny sitting-room, picking things up and putting them down again somewhere else. By the time he had finished, he'd rearranged everything in the small room. Hadn't he managed quite well since Nancy had taken bad? Molly pointed out he couldn't be in two places at the one time. No, it was no trouble, she would stay, get the older children, Mary and Joe, off to school in the morning.

When he returned from work they'd discuss what was for the best. God forbid, she couldn't leave the place in the state it was in; it wasn't fit for Nancy to return to if they discharged her from hospital. She thought: that Harry's daft as a brush.

Molly Larkin was still stiff an hour after rising. It was a good enough chair as chairs go but it wasn't the greatest bed. She might just as well tidy up before the children came down for their breakfast. Poor mites. Her own were all grown-up now, gone from home, making their own way in the world. She hadn't noticed Harry leave on his milk round, but he must have passed her on his way out.

While she busied herself, Molly wondered what had happened to Nancy's baby. She was sure Nancy hadn't harmed it. She knew, of course, about baby-blues and cot deaths, but the baby had been exceptionally lusty, and although Nancy had seemed harassed at times and the house a bit chaotic, she didn't seem to Molly to have been really low. Molly was very suspicious of Harry's indifference to the child's disappearance; he was more disturbed about his missing watch. She made up her mind to visit Nancy as soon as possible.

Joe and Mary came down morning-eyed.

'What you doing here?' Mary fiddled with a button on her cardigan as she glanced up at Molly.

'Just helping out till your mum gets out of hospital.' Molly placed the milk on the table.

'Why's my mum in hospital?'

'She's just had a bit of a turn. She'll be fine soon, you'll see. She'll be home again before you know it,' she said hurriedly.

She no-nonsensed the children through their breakfast porridge, then brushed their hair and inspected their hands and teeth. She felt bad every time she evaded their direct questions. As she hurried them out of the front door she said, a touch too severely: 'Mind you work hard at school today. Give your mum reason to be proud of you and she'll return home all the quicker.' God love them, she thought . 'And mind the traffic.' She waved and turned hastily, lest they should sense the spike of fear she felt, see the tear in her eye.

'Molly Larkin, you're a fool!' she said to herself, as she

11

glanced round the empty room, and turned up the radio. A tango. her favourite. She hoisted up her skirt into her bloomers, got down on all fours, and set to with alacrity. Boom-boom-boom-boom, cha-cha-cha-cha-cha, boom-boom-boom-boom, cha-cha-cha-cha-cha; she polished the floor in time to the music. She chuckled to herself as she considered that someone might just peep through the window.

Edith clung to Martha, who was sucking her fist with concentrated desperation. Arnold dressed and shaved, while he absorbed the truth of Martha's arrival.

'Dear, I shall go and report the matter to the police. I think it would be best if you kept the baby here while I find out what is the right thing to do.' Arnold put on his coat. 'I don't think we should take the little thing out, it might catch cold, and in any case I'm not sure what they would do with it at the police station.'

While Arnold was gone, Edith warmed some milk, added a little sugar, tested the temperature on the back of her hand, as she had seen her mother do a long time ago, and attempted to push spoonfuls into Martha's mouth. But the baby's tongue kept pushing the spoon away. By the time Arnold returned with P.C. Newman, the baby was very wet down the front, and underneath for that matter, and she was crying. It took great restraint from Edith not to weep too.

The policeman wrote down the details, such as they were, and took charge of the shopping-basket for evidence. The doctor and the district nurse arrived. They all inspected Martha, who was crying with great lusty gulps now, and the district nurse left hurriedly, returning with a bottle, teat, and a tin of dried milk.

They agreed, and she acquiesced, that Edith should take

care of the baby; it would be so much better than taking it to hospital, where it might pick up something. The policeman left to make enquiries and inform the Press. Edith had a silent hope, but it made her feel guilty.

Harry set off, after his round, to report the loss of his watch to the police station. It was not the kind of thing he would normally have been inclined to do; but he was aware of its value. It was a reminder of his grandfather (of whom he had been very fond), and would be worth a few quid if he needed it in an emergency.

The walk to the station gave him an opportunity to consider what to do; the doctor in the hospital had hinted darkly that Nancy might have done something with the baby. He didn't want her put away, but couldn't very well implicate himself in its disappearance. Harry boy, he said to himself, you've got yourself in a right old pickle; and he kicked a stone into the gutter and watched the dust rise.

Edith did very well managing Martha, considering her lack of experience, and Arnold was impressed whenever he watched her coping with all the messy things that have to be done with babies. She, who always took such an interest in church matters and involved herself whenever she could, was too occupied with the little baby to create her usual miracles of efficient organization during the Easter ceremonies.

After four days, Edith, lulled into complacency, was surprised when P.C. Newman called to report no progress in the hunt for the baby's parents. As he left, something bright caught his attention. He bent down and extricated a pocket-watch caught in the lavender bush beside the front door. He offered it to Arnold as he came up the garden path. At Arnold's disclaimer, he nodded his head and put it carefully into his pocket.

'Someone must have dropped it.' He looked back at the lavender bush. 'I'll pop into Lost Property and make enquiries.' He took the watch out again, and two of his braincells accidentally collided. 'Of course, it might be important evidence!' And he turned it over, wound it, put it to his ear, and looked at it for several seconds, before replacing it in his pocket as he strode off with a wave.

'I think we should talk about the baby's future, dear. It is most vexing. It doesn't look as if anyone is going to claim her.' Arnold settled into the hard-backed armchair, and peered at Edith. A little spring of hope pushed its way to the surface. Edith smiled, and folded her hands neatly and demurely in her lap.

'The policeman said we might adopt her, dear, though of course we shall have to apply to the court. And that's only if her parents don't claim her.' Edith thought: why couldn't they just keep the baby? She and Arnold would take such good care of the dear little thing. 'Arnold, it doesn't make sense to hand her back to parents who abandoned her. People like that shouldn't be allowed to keep children.'

'We don't know the circumstances, dear, and perhaps they won't turn up, as you suggest, though it's early days yet.' But the spring was growing, lapping, lapping, flowing free, spreading itself greedily all over, flooding every little place in Edith's heart.

'Oh Arnold, she's such a happy baby, so contented with us, so absolutely perfect . . .' Edith considered. 'Her mother and father would surely have come forward by now if they'd had any intention.'

'Perhaps she doesn't have a father.'

Edith looked perturbed. How could Arnold possibly

think such a thing? 'Arnold, dear. All babies have to have a father. What are you suggesting?'

'Perhaps her parents aren't married. Sometimes girls, er, get themselves into trouble. It happened last year to one of my parishioners. We had to send her away to a girls' home to have her baby and it was adopted immediately.' And he drummed his fingers together impatiently. 'You know very well, I told you at the time. It really is the most likely explanation.'

'My dear Arnold, we cannot adopt a baby who isn't legitimate. No, no, no. It wouldn't be right to have a child of sin in the house of a man of God. It would be a bad example. Besides, if we don't know who her father is, we would be taking a terrible chance. Her father might be a criminal or something. Think of all the bad blood. At the very least he must be irresponsible. No, you cannot reward people like that by taking care of their children; it just encourages them.'

Before he left for church Arnold made the relevant arrangements. He couldn't tell if it was distress or disapproval when the district nurse sniffed as she took the baby from Edith and stepped into the ambulance. He was comforted by the policeman's assurance that parents of doorstep babies were usually traced.

'It is time,' said P.C. Newman, fumbling with something metallic in his pocket, 'to step up my inquiries.'

Edith went upstairs and locked herself in the bathroom. The four sleepless nights and additional worry and work for the baby had left her enervated – evidenced by the face that stared back at her through toothpaste splashes on the mirror. She examined herself. Yes, there was crosshatching she hadn't noticed before, and the skin around her eyes was puffy, as if she'd been crying. She felt something burning in her throat, as she bent over the basin. There was a terrible dry ache where her heart was.

Arnold turned the key in the big oak door and went up the aisle. He tried to concentrate on the Good Friday service, but couldn't progress beyond the image of someone washing hands.

Visiting hours were between two and four, but Molly didn't know if they'd let her in. She packed some fruit, a fancy bit of soap she'd received at Christmas, and her own good nightdress; well, she could at least leave them for Nancy, even if they didn't allow her to stay. Before setting off, she tidied up hastily and began to set the grate. She took an old unread newspaper and placed it on the hearth. When the first shovel of cold ashes descended, the truth shook her as she took in the headline all in one:

BABY FOUND ON DOORSTEP

She took hold of the newspaper, tipped off the ashes, read it carefully, and put it in with the nightdress and the other things.

3

HARRY ARRIVED AT the hospital clutching a bunch of flowers as Molly was leaving. He avoided anything more than a perfunctory greeting, and she tacitly concurred. There was no one in Nancy's bed, but a newspaper caught Harry's eye. Mrs Appleby was staring at him from across the ward, unblinking.

'She's gone to inspect the baby.'

'Er. . . could you explain what you mean?' Harry said, thinking to himself: the cat's out of the bag now. He placed the flowers on the bed, covering the newspaper.

'Well, of course I don't often listen to other people's conversations,' Mrs Appleby lied. 'But it's rather difficult to avoid it, actually' – she tossed her head – 'if they insist on shouting. No manners at all,' she sighed. 'Mrs Appleby was just having her afternoon snooze when a crazy woman burst in with that newspaper.' She pointed. 'And quite frightened me,' Mrs Appleby said timorously, and sighed again.

Harry affected deafness, fiddling with the flowers and hypocritically bent on smoothing Nancy's bedcover. The door opened, revealing a nurse, and Nancy, and a short, plump stethoscoped doctor. Nancy was too preoccupied with the baby in her arms to see Harry immediately.

'Ah! Mr Eagan.' The doctor smiled, advancing and waving his hand in Harry's general direction. 'Your wife seems very happy now. She's reunited with her baby. A most unusual affair. The baby was found on a doorstep four days ago. Abandoned. I'll leave her to tell you the details.' He indicated Nancy. 'I'm surprised you haven't heard it on the news, or seen the papers.' He put his hands in the pockets of his white coat. 'It's very delicate, of course – the whole episode, I mean, not the child. Sometimes women take against a baby soon after delivery. It's really quite common, though I must say this is an extreme case.' He was looking at something invisible above Harry's left shoulder. 'I have a prescription here for your wife. Something to calm her.' He handed Harry an envelope without looking at him. 'And you must take her to your G.P. as soon as possible. I have spoken to her.'

He turned, not waiting for a reply, showed his teeth to Nancy, and patted the baby, before walking swiftly to the door and shutting it behind him. Harry couldn't believe his luck. Nancy still hadn't said anything. He pushed her towards the bed, pointing to the flowers.

It wasn't light yet. There was an odd chirp though, and somewhere close at hand a lonely train moved silently and slowly through the night. It pushed its way surely and inexorably along the familiar track, shunting back and forth, before arriving at Harry's favourite destination.

'Of course we'll keep the bloody kid,' Harry replied as he pulled himself out of her and rolled over, and thought: what a time to bring it up.

Nancy had identified the baby. The nurse told her Martha had cried until her face was swollen. Nancy thought perhaps this was why she didn't recognize her, why she couldn't convince herself it was Martha. By the time she believed it was Martha, the baby was happy and contented. But that was many days later.

Edith collected all the things she had bought for the baby, and made them into a parcel. At first she considered them for the church jumble sale, but when Arnold agreed with her, she sent them down to the police station with a note.

To the mother of the Baby.
We were very privileged to have your little girl for a few days. During this time my husband and myself grew very fond of her. We read in the newspaper that you had been reunited with your daughter, but of course they didn't give your name. The police told us you are a very charming family with two older children but they could not divulge your identity. We hope you will accept the clothes and other things we bought for your baby. We would like to keep in touch with her but should not like to intrude. We have no children of our own and your baby was very precious to us for the short time we cared for her. My address is above if you would care to contact us. It would make us very happy if you did.
(signed) Mrs Edith Mellors.

Nancy and her baby sat uncomfortably in the austere waiting-room. The grey drizzling day contrasted with the dry, stuffy warmth inside. The room was quite square. A door led directly to the outside world and another to the doctor's surgery, and there was a window in one wall where the receptionist was visible. The chairs, crammed tightly together along two walls, were the only things that touched. Four people sat patiently, silently contained in invisible cages. A large, red-haired young woman came through the door and walked up to the window where the receptionist was busy writing in a book spread before her on the counter. The woman talked fast, offering her name and address and asking to see the doctor.

All eyes watched while the receptionist explained that if she hadn't registered she would have to wait for another day. No, she couldn't see the doctor without registering on the Panel; and no, not even if she did it immediately.

'But I've only just moved here,' said the woman.

'Well, my dear, you should have thought of that before.'

'But I didn't know I was going to be ill,' said the young woman desperately. 'I must see a doctor.'

'You'd better go to the casualty department then,' said the receptionist firmly, and handed her a piece of paper with the address of the hospital on it. 'Next, please.' She indicated Nancy as a patient came out of the doctor's surgery.

'It's very difficult for me to help you, Nancy, if you persist in claiming you can't remember anything about your baby's disappearance.' The doctor pushed her chair back, came from behind her desk, and sat on a chair beside Nancy.

'Listen, my dear, it isn't anything to be ashamed of. Many women have a problem with depression after they've had a baby.' She put her hand on Nancy's shoulder. 'It's very common. And she isn't harmed.' The doctor took a handkerchief from her pocket, as she saw the tears tumble down Nancy's face.

'It isn't what you think.' Nancy dabbed her eyes.

'What do you mean? Don't you want your baby? I'm sure you'll get over these feelings. With a little help.' The doctor straightened her skirt, brushing off a bit of fluff. 'I can give

20

you something to cheer you up, to help you cope. And I shall come and see you and the baby again in a couple of days.' The doctor moved back to her desk, and took out a prescription pad.

'I don't need any bloody pills. There's nothing wrong with me. Nothing.' Nancy looked fiercely at the doctor. 'I'm fed up with everyone assuming I've dumped my own baby. As if I could do such a thing.' She clutched the child closer to her.

'We cannot get away from the facts, my dear.' The doctor stopped writing.

'It wasn't me. I didn't do it.'

'Well , if you didn't abandon your baby, Nancy, who did?' The doctor leaned towards her.

'I can't tell you, because it will get someone into trouble.'

'But you must explain to me what happened. I'm your doctor, Nancy, you can confide in me, you know. I would respect your confidence; indeed, it would be quite wrong for me to repeat anything you said to me.'

'Harry did it.' Nancy's staccato voice was louder than she intended. She checked the doctor's impassive face before continuing. 'He didn't want her, because she isn't his.' Her voice was quieter. 'He couldn't bear looking at her. I think he hoped I'd just forget her and accept it if I knew she was adopted by decent people. I mean, he has a right to be angry.'

'It makes it much more serious if he is the culprit, you know. It puts me in a bit of a dilemma, Nancy.'

'Look, he knows what he did is wrong. He won't do it again. He knows he could be charged if anyone else knew what he had done. No one else knows except you . . .' She started to weep again. 'He'd kill me if he knew I'd told you. If you say anything to anyone, it will go wrong again. If you tell anyone it was Harry, I'll deny it. I'll just say it was me.'

'Now you know, I've just told you, as your doctor I shall never repeat anything you say to me, don't you?' She took out some tissues from a box on the desk. 'So dry your eyes, and let's see how we can sort this out.'

Nancy was finally convinced that the doctor would remain silent.

Martha grew imperceptibly every day. By the time she was one year old, she sat strapped into her blue wooden high chair, and clapped her hands when Harry came in from work, gurgling and smiling at him in greeting. The nearest he ever came to touching her was when he chucked her under the chin when she clapped, and she waved her arms and legs in great excitement. But he never picked her up, never threw her high in the air in his arms, never bounced her on his knee, never hugged or caressed her.

4

ON MARTHA'S FOURTH birthday, Harry arrived home at lunch time, with a large parcel. He wrapped the string around his thumb and first finger, leaving it to one side. Then he pulled the brown paper off a large cardboard box and folded the paper carefully, putting it in a drawer with the string.

He opened up one end of the cardboard container, cautiously peering into the interior. He put one strong, hairy arm inside the box and pulled out something with wheels on it. A tricycle. He pushed it around the kitchen while Nancy hushed him. She thought: he's going to ride it, and started to giggle.

'Ssh! Martha's asleep, you'll wake her. Put it back in the box.' She watched while he replaced the tricycle, unwound a roll of coloured paper and began to wrap the box. He took some tape and a rather crumpled and elaborate rosette from his pocket; it was nearly ten minutes before he was finally satisfied with the parcel.

Martha loved her present; she walked around it, touched it quickly, and withdrew her hand, placing it in the other for comfort. Finally she sat down beside it; she was unsure where to begin to open it.

Joe and Mary placed their school bags on the kitchen table and took off muddy shoes.

'If you don't want to open it, I'll do it for you.' Joe was pushing the parcel with his foot, and pulling at the rosette.

They couldn't get her off the tricycle once she was on it; she rode around the kitchen table. She gave Harry a shy and sticky kiss in thanks, but he was hovering, ready to take off as she flew past him every few seconds on her circular adventure to nowhere.

Molly pushed her chestnut hair back with a well-used brush. Merciful hour, she thought, Molly Larkin, you've a good few lines, and some of them have riven undesirable, unscheduled routes. And she peered at her face in the mirror. Who was it, she thought, who'd said you have the face you deserve at fifty? Silly really, it implied that you could give credit to people who'd had an easy life. She put a bottle of home-made wine into a paper bag. She must hand it discreetly to Nancy; she didn't want it falling into Harry's eager hands.

The uneasiness between herself and Harry was exacerbated by his suspicion that Molly knew the truth about the free-give-away he'd attempted when he'd delivered Martha with the milk nearly four years ago. But, for Nancy's peace of mind, Molly didn't tell anyone of her secret suspicions, and that included indicating to Harry that she was ignorant of the truth.

She took a deep breath, in anticipation of Harry's antipathy towards her, which usually took the form of a sort of grey look which descended on him whenever she entered the house. She knocked on the door as she opened it.

'Ah Molly, how are you?' Harry obsequiously offered her a chair. No doubt he was behaving like this because she'd agreed to babysit when Nancy had asked her, but she found it as distasteful as his hostility.

'I got a bit of a rise today,' he said. 'We're celebrating.'

They'd had a few drinks when, perched on the pub stool, Nancy shifted her weight from one buttock to the other, undid her coat, put her hands together, and leaned forward.

'It means a lot to me, you being so kind to Martha today.' She pulled her unbuttoned coat around her.

'A birthday is important,' he said, putting down his beer. 'And it'll keep her occupied.' He punched the table with his fist before reaching again for his drink. 'Look how we couldn't drag her off it.' He drained his glass.

'Let me get the next one.' She was already rummaging in her bag.

'I never let a woman buy me anything, you know that.' He folded his arms.

'I'd like to get you something, you being so generous today and so on.' She snapped her bag shut.

'You're saying I'm not like that usually. Is that what you mean? Tight-fisted. Is that what you think of me?' He leaned across the table until his face was inches away from hers. 'You're stupid.'

'If you're going to start that, I'm going home.' She was already buttoning her coat. 'You're always the same after a few drinks.'

'Sit down. You're a kill-joy. Bloody great, isn't it? I take you out for the night, and you want to leave after a couple of drinks.' There was a ball of saliva at the corner of his mouth. 'You're soft, daft. If you didn't have Martha, you could go out to work yourself, you know.' He was shaking his head and pawing the ground. 'I've been generous, you say, and then you want to repay me by getting me a drink. Out of money I've given you. You got a pair of scales where your brain should be.' And he stood up to get another drink.

'Paying for the drinks doesn't give you the right to insult me.' Nancy gulped down a quarter of hers as she watched him place another on the table and sit down. 'I'd like it if I could give you something. That's all.'

'You give me plenty, girl.' Harry grinned, bent over and tapped her leg.

Edith placed two pots of home-made jam in the bag with Martha's present. Every year she visited the Little Family on the child's birthday. This year she had knitted Martha a jumper, with great patience, a lot of time, and not much skill. But it will look all right when it is on, she thought. Arnold worried that their intentions might be misinterpreted; he knew that the family were not parishioners, but each year so far he'd bidden them farewell at the end of the annual visit with the automatic 'See you on Sunday at Service, then.' He always tried to stop the tape but it went on rolling anyway; this time he must concentrate, and remember not to start it.

Arnold noticed that Edith was agitated; her mouth was working away silently, twisting and moving up and down, as she dried and polished the dishes. He picked at a bit of dried supper which had landed on his cardigan, and cleaned his pipe for the second time that day.

'It's nearly six o'clock, dear, I really think we should leave soon.'

'Don't fuss, Arnold dear, I've nearly finished.' A plate crashed to the ground. 'Now look what's happened.' Arnold bent down with the dustpan and brush. 'Give it to me, dear, you never do it properly.' She took the dustpan and brush from him.

The door of the old car squeaked as he opened it for her. He steered clear as she strode purposefully towards it, clutching her umbrella and bag of gifts.

'I must shut the gate, dear.' She turned abruptly, marched towards the gate, stumbled on the wet pavement beside the railings next to the gate, stopped, looked for a second at her wrist, and returned to the car.

'Ready now?' He looked at her sitting beside him and then glanced in the rear-view mirror.

'Yes. Er . . . I have a hole in my arm,' she said quietly.

'Right. We'd better get started.' Arnold turned the key.

'Dear, I don't think you heard me. I have a hole in my wrist. I impaled it on a railing,' she said loudly.

Arnold stared at the offered wrist incredulously. He was looking at the inside of Edith. There was no blood, but little white tendons, that looked exceedingly like thin worms, around the inside edge of the hole.

His hands shook as he drove to the casualty department.

Molly settled her small parlour; gave the marigolds some water, plumped up the cushions, put the cat out with a soothing stroke. Her book lay beside the bedside lamp. Her slow, deliberate calmness would have shown, to anyone who cared to observe her, a sad acceptance; nobody did. Molly considered how fortunate she was not to have to confront the turmoil evidently raging next door. She found it hard to concentrate on her book while she lay comfortably reading in bed. The noises she could hear through the thin wall were predictable, considering the sweaty appearance of Harry when he and Nancy had returned at closing time. Then she heard a car draw up outside.

There was a battle raging in Harry's head too. When he

27

heard the car stop he opened the front door abruptly, and a sudden rush of cold air hit him. Steadying himself against the door frame he blinked twice as he stared at two people standing on the doorstep. One appeared to him to be wounded.

'I'm sorry to call so late, but my wife has hurt her arm.'

'I'm not a bleeding doctor, mate.' Harry tried unsuccessfully to focus.

'I know. I wonder if we could just come in for a minute.'

'You want to use a 'phone to get help? We don't have one here.' Harry belched.

'We've come with Martha's birthday present. Er . . . perhaps we'll call again tomorrow. I'm really most sorry we have disturbed you at this late hour, but Edith would, er . . . insist; she said it was important. For the little one's sake, you understand.' He was shuffling his weight from one foot to the other and looking at Edith. 'My wife has had an accident coming here, and we spent several hours waiting in casualty . . . She was anxious, you know.'

'Reverend! Do come in. I'm sorry, I didn't recognize you immediately.' Harry stared at Arnold's collar. 'I've had a very tiring day.'

'Thank you,' Arnold said as he held Edith's good elbow, guiding her inside.

'Reverend, please do sit down. And your good lady.' Harry bowed as he pulled out the chairs for them.

'We've brought your little girl a little something.' Edith smiled and placed the bag on the table and extracted a parcel. 'For Martha.' She handed it to Harry.

'Not another of those horrible things you made for her last year, surely?' Harry grinned at Edith, who shrugged her shoulders and smiled nervously in return.

'Yes!' she squeaked. 'I do hope it fits.' She delved into the bag again to fetch out the jam.

'We got enough horrible things in this house already.' Harry looked triumphant. 'Hundreds of horrible things. We probably got more horrible things than anyone else in the world.' He swept his arms around as he saw Nancy descend the stairs. 'Horrible people too.'

Arnold stood up as she came towards the table. Edith pushed the parcel towards Nancy. 'For Martha, a birthday present,' she said awkwardly. 'I'm sorry to call so late, but I had an accident.' She waved her arm in its sling. 'I know how important birthdays are to children.' She slid the jars of jam a little closer to Nancy.

'Thank you very much, it's very kind of you to think of Martha. Oh, and I'm sorry you've hurt your arm, I hope it isn't serious.' Nancy moved closer to the table. 'I'm sure we'll all enjoy the jam too, very thoughtful of you.'

'Just something I . . .' began Edith, but the movement of Harry folding his arms caught her eye. 'It's very late, I know, we must be going.' She picked up her bag.

'Come to have a look at how the poor live, eh?' Harry placed both hands on the table and bent towards Edith. 'Have a good look then. We're a dying breed. Ha, ha.'

'Steady on,' Arnold intervened. 'We only . . .'

'Who asked you to interrupt, Reverend? You come into my bloody house, at some god-awful hour' – Edith winced – 'with bleeding pots of jam,' Harry continued. 'Makes you feel good, does it? Here's what I think of your bloody jam.' His hand crashed down on the table before sweeping across it.

Edith got up, her mouth working overtime as she watched a sobbing Nancy pick up the mess of glass and red stuff.

Arnold pushed Edith gently towards the door, placing himself between her and Harry. He opened his mouth, but Harry beat him to it.

'Christ!' Harry was holding his head in his hands. 'I got the fucking sack today, and I've spent most of my redundancy money. I'm bloody redundant,' he shouted, and looked nervously at Nancy. 'I didn't get a rise. They're laying people off. I thought we'd have one last good night out. A good time. There'll be plenty of rough ones ahead.'

Everyone else left or went to bed. Harry poured the last from a beer bottle into a glass. He took a label from the drawer and examined it. In capital letters, beside 'TO:', he wrote 'RUBBISH', and below, beside 'FROM:', he wrote 'RUBBISH'. From under the table, he took out the big cardboard box that had contained the tricycle and which Martha had turned into a little house for herself. He opened the drawer again. He noticed sweat drip on to the brown paper as he removed it, and the string, and placed them on the table.

He went quietly upstairs; he had one last birthday surprise for Martha. He laid her over his shoulder as he carried her downstairs.

'Look , little Miss Nuisance.' He laid her limp body on the table. He said, showing her the label, 'I'm sending you away.' Martha looked startled. 'The postman will deliver you to someone else.'

In the beginning she thought Harry was playing a game. After all, she had used the box for her play-house that afternoon. She whimpered as her elbow caught in a window Nancy had cut out of her cardboard house. She heard the crisp rustle of the brown paper as he wrapped her up in the box, the sound of the string and the thud of his hand as he slapped on the label. She heard the tearing sound of the tape as he unwound it and bound the box. She felt him lift the box and carry it down the street. He left it outside the post office.

5

MARTHA OPENED HER eyes as wide as she could but still couldn't see anything. She stretched out and thrust her head upwards. There was a slight but unyielding give but she couldn't get out. Her nose was blocked, so she opened her mouth, but couldn't breathe. She could hear gulping. Her chest felt as if someone was sitting on it. Her head was bursting with pain. Her teeth and tongue were too big for her mouth. Her limbs felt fat and pudgy and though she was shivering, her skin was burning. She was growing, her body filling every inch of the container she was in, squashing itself and pouring into the corners. She felt spikes in her stomach, smelled something sharp and putrid, and a liquid warmth slid down between her thighs. She tried to fling her arms and legs out and felt her whole world roll over.

The parcel somersaulted across the pavement into the gutter. Water seeped slowly through the box and muffled wailing came from it.

Fireman Chris wearily nursed the tender home after a false alarm. He caught sight of the rolling parcel, which elicited an automatic response. The brakes of the fire tender squealed as he kicked his foot down hard on the pedal. Curiosity determined his investigation. He was first out of the cab.

Chris bent down, extended his arms but kept his head turned away slightly while he lifted the noisy package back onto the pavement. He turned the parcel on end, tearing the paper, and clawing urgently at the cardboard. His great hands enveloped Martha's head to guide and deliver her, wet, wriggling, bawling, shivering, and stinking out into the cold night.

'Jesus! I thought at worst it was a dog.' The others were out of the tender now; a blanket was handed across to Chris, who wrapped it around Martha.

'Get an ambulance, mate.' Chris cradled the bleating child in his big arms, stroked her hair gently from her face, and rocked her while they waited.

'What's your name?' he whispered.

Information about Martha was recorded on various printed forms, by the hospital, police, and Social Services department, and then filed away. Martha herself was to be filed away in 'a place of safety': a Residential Council Home.

'This isn't my home,' she said as they arrived on the damp afternoon of her admittance. You'd think they would know after all the questions I've answered, she thought.

'Now, you know, Martha, I've explained it to you. You won't be going back to your old home just yet. You have a new one now,' said Auntie Helen.

'Oh.'

'You'll like it here. Lots of other children. And you'll meet your special auntie in a minute. Come on' – she opened the front door – 'and we'll have a chat with her.' She wiped her shoes on the mat. 'She'll want to know all about you.'

Arnold placed a morning paper and a gift-wrapped oblong package on the table and stared at Edith for a few seconds. He coughed.

'A present for you, dear.'

'It's not my birthday.' Edith was in no mood for frivolities. 'What a terrible man.'

'Oh, I don't know dear, I think you're overstating it a bit. I'm not so bad.' Arnold put his hands in his pockets.

'Don't be silly, Arnold. I mean Mr Eagan. His dreadful behaviour last night!' She shook her head. 'And that poor woman; what she must have to tolerate, I can't imagine. The child shouldn't be in an environment like that. Drunken father. Out of work. Think of the frightful damage his influence will do on the fragile, developing personality of that sweet child. What can we do?'

'What do you suggest is feasible?' Arnold lit his pipe, holding a matchbox over the top as he sucked at it.

'We should have kept her when we had the opportunity.' Edith snapped her mouth shut.

'My dear, that would have been kidnapping. The church doesn't recommend such activities for the reclamation or salvation of souls.' He stared out of the window.

'I've made up my mind. If we cannot do anything to help her – and it is clear that we cannot – then I shall not risk submitting myself again to such abusive behaviour by visiting the family any more. We shall have to content ourselves with remembering them in our prayers.' Edith picked up the package and began to unwrap the chocolates.

'I want to wee.' Martha pulled her hand away from Auntie Helen. 'Now!' she shouted.

'All right. Come on then. We'll meet Auntie Susan after you've been. Follow me and I'll show you the way.' She went down a corridor, pushing Martha ahead.

Martha gazed at the long row of lavatories, each in a separate cubicle. The doors were open except one. There was a gap at the top and bottom of the closed door. Why had they got so many? Which one should she choose? She wanted to go too urgently to speculate for long.

She hauled herself up on one, leaving the door open.

For a long time Martha would not allow anyone to shut a door. She could manage a scream pitched around the threshold of intolerable pain. All the staff wondered at such a small child managing to emit so large a noise. They were patient, firm, and controlled. Gradually Martha allowed them to shut the door for a little while. Then longer each time. But she often sneaked over and opened it again.

Auntie Susan bent over the seated child at her desk and placed her hand over Martha's. She guided the smaller hand over the page as she formed the words, 'Love, Martha.'

'That's good, Martha.' Auntie Susan picked up the page and admired it. 'Your mum will be happy when she gets this.'

'Will she get it soon? Today?' Martha got off the chair, opened the door and walked back and sat down, again.

'No. She'll get it tomorrow.'

'Will she send me a letter, do you think?'

'Of course she will.'

'Will she send it today?'

'No, tomorrow, I expect.'

'I've never had a letter before. I'll get one today. No, I'll get one tomorrow.'

'No, you'll get one the day after.'

'When's that?'

'I can't have her back.' Nancy's pinched face looked nervously at Molly. 'It's not that I don't want her. Of course, I do.' She picked up Joe's shirt and laid it over the ironing-board, straightening the back with her hand. 'But what can I do?'

'You're irreplaceable. There's no one in the world like you, to her. The little pet. She's no trouble and she has lovely little ways. Nancy . . .' Molly shook her head slowly, 'think hard, girl, before you make such a moment-ous decision.'

'I have. You must know that. When he dumped her before, and everyone, except you, thought I'd done it, I had a hold on him. He had to behave himself because he was afraid I'd tell the truth. Well, the doctor knew, but Harry didn't know that.' She drew the iron across the shirt. 'Now, he has nothing to lose because he's been caught.' She was poking the iron into the corners around the neck. 'And he'll never settle as long as Martha's around. And also . . .' She set the iron down firmly on end and looked at Molly. 'I've got the other two to think of.'

'It's either him or her, then?'

'You're being a bit hard, aren't you? He might get off with a fine or probation or something. Then we'll be a family again. It's his first offence.' Nancy blew her nose but the tears still came.

'First one he's been caught for, you mean.' Molly folded her arms. 'Are you really sure what you're doing, letting her go?'

'They said I could visit her. They encourage parents to

35

keep in touch.' Nancy sniffed and folded the shirt. 'If I had her back he'd do it again and then he'd end up behind bars.'

'Lord!' Molly said, putting on her coat. 'That's a fine irony. Harry behind bars.' And her laughter drifted into every corner of the room. Molly saw a smile lift the corner of Nancy's mouth. 'He spends more time inside bars than any publican himself.'

Auntie Helen handed out the morning post the day after. Martha watched her as she made her way down the opposite side of the long table. She turned and walked down Martha's side, and hesitated as she slid behind the child. She put two letters down on the table between Billy and Martha.

'You'll trip someone up leaving your chair out like that,' said Auntie Helen as she pushed Martha's chair in and then, lifting the precious letters again, she proceeded down to the end of the table.

'Can I have the rest of your toast?' Billy grinned at Martha, moving his hand slowly towards her plate.

'No.'

'Thanks very much,' Billy said as he gave her a hefty kick on the ankle, lifting the slice smoothly on to his own plate.

Billy had been in residential care all his life. Longer, in this Home, than anyone else. It was his responsibility to be Martha's Special Friend. Look after her. Show her around. Help her settle down. Make her feel at home. He was seven.

She followed him to the room he slept in. While he put on his outdoor shoes, she held on to the door handle.

'Why are you staring at me?' Billy tried unsuccessfully to tie his lace. 'I can nearly do it by myself.'

'Um,' said Martha, swinging one leg.

'What's the matter with you? Lost your tongue?'

'I'm cross.'

'Why?'

'I want a letter.'

'You can have one of my old ones if you like. I got a card in an envelope somewhere.' He got up, shoe laces trailing, and rummaged through a drawer, spilling things onto the floor. 'Here.' Half the contents of the drawer followed him as he sloped over to Martha. 'I got it for my birthday. But you can cross my name out. And I'll write yours on it for you.'

'Billy?' Martha put the envelope on his bed.

'What?' His eyes followed her hand.

'Are you my brother?'

'No.'

'Well, why are your aunties my aunties then?'

'They're everyone's bleedin' aunties. I mean, they're not really anyone's aunties. Well, they may be. But they're not anyone's aunties that lives here, silly. They just like us to call them that. Dunno why.' His eyes were on the envelope. 'If you don't want that card, give it back.'

'I want a letter,' – Martha bit her lip – 'from my mum.'

6

THE LONG, FLAT sofas in the communal room backed up against the wall; sitting down she felt she was waiting for someone.

'School,' said Billy, 'is a right doss.' He stood in front of Martha. 'You'll like it, honest,' he said, offering her his already chewed gum. She shook her head. 'It's only chewed once. You know, one time round the mouth.'

'Don't be disgusting, Billy. Take it away. Your shoe-laces are undone. You'll trip over them.' Martha swung her feet under the sofa.

'Who?' Billy turned his head and looked ostentatiously behind him. 'Who you talking to? There's no one else here.'

'You. Look!' She pointed.

'Saves time getting ready for bed.'

'What are you two doing?' Annie dumped the vacuum cleaner down. 'The school bus has arrived. They'll be looking for you. Come on.' She aimed them towards the door. 'Billy Watts! Will you never tidy yourself!' She knelt down and tied his laces, double-knotting them. 'There now.' She got up and bent so that her face was level with his. 'I've got to clean this room' – she looked around her – 'and I can't do it with you hanging around.'

'Where do you live?' Martha tugged Annie's arm, delaying her departure by taking her time as she picked up her satchel.

'Linton Street. Not far from here. About ten minutes' walk.'

'Oh!' Martha pulled the satchel over her shoulder. 'Do you have any children?'

'No. What would I want with children, with all you lot to clean up after?' She steered Billy by the shoulder towards the door again. 'Off!'

'Wait, Martha!' Annie was foraging in the large pocket of her overall. 'Here.'

'A book!' said Martha. 'But I can't read.'

'You'll learn to read at school,' she said. 'This book is about myths and legends.' She delved into her pocket again. Something hard hit the lollies as she lifted them out of her pocket. She saved the small bottle as it nearly fell to the floor. 'Annie's medicine,' she smiled. 'Here' – she handed the lollies to Martha – 'There's one for you, for good luck, on your first day at school.' She whispered, close to her ear, 'And one for him' – she nodded towards the departing figure – 'if he behaves himself.'

He didn't. She gave it to him anyway.

'Your mother is coming to see you,' said Auntie Susan as Martha skipped through the door. She stopped.

'When?'

'Today.'

'Is she coming to take me home?'

'No. She's coming to see you. So go up and change your shoes and brush your hair. Your face could do with a wash too.'

39

Nancy was ill at ease. 'It's nice here,' she said, looking around the room. Martha walked to the door, opened it, and returned quickly to her mother. 'Nice curtains' – she glanced towards the window – 'and a carpet. Very nice.'

'Can I sit on your knee?'

"Course you can.' She helped her up, then leaned behind the sofa and ran her fingers along the radiator. 'Central heating! In October! Such extravagance!'

'I want to come home with you.' Martha snuggled into Nancy, burrowing her head into her soft breasts.

'Who's that funny lady you sitting on?' A shout from the open door made Martha turn. A group of children was pushing, shouting, and staring. Martha slid off Nancy's knee and shoved the door shut as a passing auntie yanked some of the kids away. Auntie Susan brought in a tea tray. She settled herself beside Nancy and told her that Martha had been good at school. Sometime in the future, they agreed, Martha could go home for a visit. It was a bleak promise.

When Nancy got up to leave, Martha clawed at her, trying to hold on. Auntie Susan helped to pull Martha off. Little girls who don't let their mother go, and cry when they leave, won't see them so often. Nancy was broken by the incident, too overwhelmed with guilt and inadequacy to repeat the experience. She sent Martha Christmas and birthday presents, but she never visited her again. Though she received the obligatory letters home from Martha, she didn't reply.

Martha's life was filled with aunties, school, Annie, Billy, and lots of other kids. Some stayed a short time, and some, like Billy, remained. When Billy learned to tie his laces he put the skill to use.

Frank Hawkins lived alone in a neat bachelor pad near

Martha and Billy's school, where he taught. He was a gregarious, volatile man, who could be exceptionally generous when in the mood.

Near the end of the school day Frank Hawkins was impatient because he looked forward to his flirtation with Auntie Susan. Trouble was, he liked her. His problem lay in the intense shyness which overcame him when making overtures towards any woman who wasn't a stranger. He planned to take the school bus back to the Home with the blasted kids and have a little chat with Auntie Susan about Billy. The difficulty would be to change gear plausibly and as soon as possible: to slide the discussion away from Billy, and around to Auntie Susan. He was breathing faster as he chalked up the final few words on to the blackboard. With unfocused eyes he sat down and faced the blur of the classroom. He missed seeing Billy drop his rubber over the edge of the desk. It didn't register when the child bent down to spend some time retrieving it.

The class were copying down the words on the blackboard. A white chiffon cloud enveloped Susan's head as he pulled up her gown, covering her face; she released her arms and slid manicured hands across his torso as the bell rang.

Blink, blink, went Frank. He surveyed the room, swallowing hard. A snigger from the back of the classroom froze as his eyes darted along the rows. One missing. The little bugger had been here at the beginning of the lesson; where was he now? Must have sneaked out.

'Where's Billy Watts?' he asked the class in general, radar face scanning heads. The class was beginning to fidget. 'Nobody leaves until I get an answer.'

'Here, Sir.' A hand shot up followed by the rest of grubby Billy. 'Lost me rubber, Sir.'

'*What!*' Frank shouted as an image of a prophylactic rose before him.

'Lost me rubber, Sir. I found it now.'

Hawkins looked at his watch. 'Class' – he scratched his head – 'put your books away before you leave.'

Billy didn't have long to laugh over the children whose shoes he'd tied together. Hawkins grabbed him. 'I'll get you, Billy Watts, just you wait,' he said, spit spraying into Billy's face, his fingers digging into his arm. 'Wait for me outside. I'm coming back in the bus with you.'

Frank went to the staff washroom to smarten himself before his confrontation with Auntie Susan. He could see the room was empty, though the lavatory door was shut. He leered lop-sidedly and admiringly at his reflection in the washroom mirror as he combed his hair. 'You're a good-looking hunk.' He straightened his tie. 'How could anyone resist you?' he said to himself as he flexed his arms, and puffed up his chest, turning sideways for a better view. 'Who's a pretty boy, then?' He winked at his reflection in the mirror to get the effect, and heard a cistern flush. He coloured as the headmaster swung out of the lavatory.

'Steady on, old chap,' said the Head, as he went towards the basin. 'Control yourself, old man.'

Six years old, Martha could make her own bed, with 'hospital corners'. Some nights she would creep out in the dark and tuck in the sheets and blankets so tightly that the mattress curved up each side to form a cradle. Most nights she could hear Billy in the next room banging his head against the wall.

She woke one morning feeling sick and hot. She could smell the wet sheet. If she stayed in bed perhaps it would dry itself. She knew she would be in trouble; that everyone else would know if the wet sheet were discovered. They'd call her 'baby'. Auntie Susan came in and felt Martha's head and said, 'Yes, poor child, there is something wrong with you. Stay here while I get a thermometer.' She hurried off.

'What's wrong with you, love?' Annie placed the broom against the wall and stood beside a sleepy Martha's bed.

'I'm sick.'

'Well, hop out a minute, and I'll freshen your bed.' She pulled back the covers. 'Put a dressing-gown around you while you sit on that chair' – she pointed – 'and we'll make you feel better.' But Martha was tugging the covers back away from Annie.

'It's not your job to make the beds.' Martha was frantic, near to tears. 'I'm old enough to make my own.'

Annie's final pull had the covers back. She glanced towards the offending sheet, scooped Martha up, and wrapped a dressing-gown around her before depositing her firmly and gently in the chair. 'Never mind,' she smiled. 'It happens to everyone sometime' – she winked – 'especially if they're feeling poorly.' Annie changed the sheets, and Martha's nightdress. She bundled the wet things together and took them away, placing them in the muddle of unsorted laundry downstairs.

'I hope I don't miss the school outing because I'm sick.'

'You'll be better by then. It's weeks away.' She puffed up the child's pillow. 'When I was a young girl I had lovely red curls, lashings of them!' She brushed Martha's hair. 'Beautiful they were, if I say so myself. I used to live in a grand house, grand it was.' She put down the brush. 'And now look at me, taking care of the likes of you.' She smiled at Martha as she placed the pillow behind her head and straightened up the covers. 'Aren't you grand now?'

'Thanks,' said Martha. 'What's grand?'

'You know very well. Oh, I used to sing and dance in the old days.'

'What did you sing?'

'Lots of old songs. I wanted to go on the stage. To sing

43

and dance. But I can sing you a song.' Martha nodded. 'What would you like?'

'I don't know. I don't know any songs.'

'Well then, I'll choose for you. And then you are to settle down and get some rest. You'll get better faster then.' And she stepped from the bed, pushed her hair up, and pinned it against her head with a comb.

'We'll gather lilacs in the spring again,' she began in a warm, powerful voice.

'This won't get the place cleaned up,' said Susan, coming through the door. 'It's very nice, Annie, but you have more important things to do.' Susan picked up the broom from the wall and handed it to Annie.

7

SHARDS OF MORNING sunlight slipped between the carelessly closed curtains onto the face of the sleeping child.
Martha stretched, arms above her head, eyes clenched, as
her mind grasped the first conscious thought. The sea-side.
Today. She moved quickly, sliding out of bed and quietly
into her clothes, before anyone else woke.

She climbed on to a chair beside the window, pulled back
the curtains, and watched a bird pecking at something in
the grass. A fly, trapped inside, butted the window in an
attempt to escape. The catch on the window was stiff, and
her little fingers worked at it, until it suddenly swung open,
nearly tossing her out. She bruised her elbow saving
herself, but excitement prevented her crying. As she
jumped down from the chair, Auntie Susan came through
the door ready to wake the children.

'Good-morning, mischief, what are you up to?' Susan
hugged her before closing the window.

'Sea-side today.' Martha clapped her hands.

'Yes, sea-side today.'

Traditionally, social workers from the Home were given

45

first option on any extra seats on the school-trip coach. Susan had accepted Frank's invitation to accompany the children, himself, and another teacher on the trip to Brighton.

Frank put on his favourite brown corduroy jacket over a lambs-wool sweater. He tucked a flat, brown-papered package under his arm, before bouncing out of his flat on his way to school.

Once there, he boarded the coach and they set off to the Home to collect Susan, Martha and a couple more children from her class who lived there.

'Morning, sweetheart,' he said to a surprised Martha. 'I'm not your teacher today, I'm your friend,' he explained, as he hoisted her on to the bottom step of the coach.

'Everyone ready?' he inquired of the group of adults and children. Martha sat down. 'Come on, up you go.' He plopped another child on to the coach.

Annie turned her bicycle into the driveway and pushed it around the side of the coach before parking it among the row of children's bikes.

'I gotta say good-bye to Annie.' Martha pushed her way down the aisle against the traffic of kids looking for seats.

'Hurry up. We're leaving in two minutes.' Frank helped her down onto the tarmac. Annie turned away from her bicycle. Martha slipped her small hand into a larger one.

'You didn't say good-bye to me,' said Martha.

'I'm here to say good-bye now.'

'I don't want to go. I want to stay with you.' Martha looked down, swinging one leg.

'Two weeks ago you were afraid you'd miss the trip because you were ill.' Annie's right hand was in her pocket. 'You know you'll have a grand time. Both her hands were behind her back. 'Which one?' she said.

46

'That one.' Martha pointed to the right. Annie brought her hand round and placed a large foil-covered chocolate biscuit in Martha's.

'Off you go. Enjoy yourself.' She led the child to the waiting coach. 'I'll still be here when you get back. You can tell me about the great time you've had then.'

Auntie Susan hoisted Martha up and over her lap on to the seat next to the window and her own.

'Has Annie been spoiling you again?' Susan was looking at the chocolate biscuit. Martha nodded.

The coach moved away. She stopped nibbling the biscuit long enough to wave to Annie. She turned back to concentrate on biting off all the chocolate around the edge before eating the inside. Quite a lot ended up on her face. Susan made her lick the corner of a cotton handkerchief before she used it to clean Martha's face. The warmth and rhythm of the coach sent the child to sleep, propped up against Susan's arm.

Frank, sitting in the seat directly in front of her, turned around, and noticing the dozing child, stared unblinking at Susan's mouth.

'You're looking like a knock-out today.' He grinned, eyes moving up to hers.

'Don't be ridiculous.' Susan felt perspiration filtering through the skin above her lips. She wiped the back of her hand across her upper lip. There was a mixture of sweat and lipstick streaks on her hand. She took the chocolate-stained handkerchief and wiped her hand, and then scrubbed it over her mouth in an attempt to remove the smeared lipstick. Frank kept watching.

'I like women' – he leaned over and stretched towards her, whispering – 'who look like tarts.' He grinned, eyes riveted to her rubbed-red mouth. 'How would you like' – he turned about him to check no one was listening – 'a nice big wet juicy kiss?'

'I've got T.B.,' she lied. 'Highly contagious,' she said regaining her composure.

'I'm going to be sick,' whimpered a white-faced child from the back of the coach. Frank shot out of his seat, grabbed the child, held him by the shoulders at arms' length, as if he were carrying a sack of rubbish, and ran with him to the front of the coach.

'Can you stop? Now! Sick child,' Frank barked over his shoulder to the driver. 'Hold on, sonny, hold on, just a minute.' The coach stopped. The door yawned open. Frank carried the child out. Martha, wakened by the jolt of the halted coach, stared out of the window at the puking child. She put her thumb in her mouth. The little boy heaved. 'It's okay, David, it's okay.' Frank was soothing him, rubbing his neck.

'Where's the sick, where's the sick?' said one of a pair of small pigtailed sisters, who ran to the door of the coach.

'Come on, back inside.' Frank had the white-faced David under his arm. He pushed the inquisitive pair back to their seats. He sat down with the sick child on his knee and wiped the cold sweat from his forehead and upper lip. He held him gently for the rest of the journey.

The coach deposited them beside the beach at Brighton. Martha spent what was left of the morning piling up stones, and avidly watching the waves roll up the beach, covering them. She ran after the sea as it receded and dared it to follow her. She backed away as wave after wave plunged towards her. Auntie Susan caught her and tried to shield her from the wind with a billowing towel, amid protestations which denied the evidence of goose-pimpled skin.

'I'm not cold.' Martha shivered.

'It's lunch-time anyway. There'll be nothing left if you

48

don't hurry.' Susan hoisted her into the air. 'Look, the picnic's all laid out.'

Martha bit into a strawberry and wiped away the saliva that dribbled down her chin. She watched a mother and a father, with two children and a baby in a pushchair, solemnly open a folding table and chairs and sit down a short distance from her. Mother heaped the plates with sandwiches and pies, while Father poured tea from a vacuum flask. The baby whinged in the pushchair until Mother handed it a bottle filled with an orange liquid.

'Want more strawberries, dreamer?'

'Yes, please.' Auntie Susan held the bowl of strawberries while Martha helped herself to more. She turned her attention towards the shore. She watched another family, a small boy and his parents, slowly climb the beach. They were all wet from swimming. The boy held his arms out, tip-toeing, trying to avoid the sharpness of the stones. A dog, dripping wet, zig-zagged after them. It stopped suddenly to shake itself.

The boy turned to call the dog. 'C'mon, fella.' The dog raced ahead, still zig-zagging, until it came to the family poised on their folding chairs around the table. Panting frantically, it stopped beside the pushchair, lifted a leg, and urinated against the wheel. Mother shrieked, Father stood up, knocking the table over, the baby dropped its bottle and wailed, the boy stood rooted to the spot, and both his parents rushed forward, attempting to apologize. Martha was fascinated – mesmerized by the confusion of half-dressed adults, with sun-burnt limbs, shouting and cursing at each other, oblivious to the dog quietly munching a pie on the ground.

'Now, children,' Frank interrupted the entertainment, 'we must pack everything away' – he indicated by spreading his arms – 'before we begin to search for shells.'

Hunting for shells did not seem to Martha an adequate substitute for the interesting domestic drama so entertainingly unfolding itself before her. Despite the fact that she hadn't been to the sea-side before, there was something vaguely familiar about this scene. Is this ordinary? she thought. Does everyone outside the Home behave in this way? she pondered, before being dragged along by the hand to join the search.

'Find as many different shells as you can.' Frank handed out paper bags to each child. 'When we get back to school we'll draw them and we'll identify them. Remember. . .' – he held aloft the flat brown package and tapped it – 'there's a prize for the biggest variety; the person who finds the most different ones.'

Martha had three shells in her bag already. She turned her back in the direction of the two squabbling families. She knew she shouldn't wander far from the school group and was afraid to do so anyway. She looked up as a seagull dived low over her head before perching on the high wall beside her. The wall helped to shelter her from the wind, which she was beginning to feel. She squatted, apparently looking for shells, but actually keeping her eyes on the families. To her disappointment they wandered off in different directions, the one lot scolding the dog and the other packing away their picnic with aggressive deliberation and Mother shaking her head.

The beach was quiet, except for the noise of the sea. The other children were occupied with their hunt for shells. Martha added two more dark-coloured open shells to her collection. The sun began to prickle the back of her neck. She wiped a sandy hand across her neck and felt the heat from it. She was thirsty.

There was a large boulder just two feet in front of her, adjacent to the wall. She bent forward, and peered over the top. A tiny bird lay on its side behind the boulder, one eye staring up at her. She leant back again so that the bird was out of view and put a sandy thumb in her mouth. Back again, bending over the boulder, she gently scooped up the bird. A wing fluttered. She dropped it. It rolled stiffly over on its back, both feet in the air. One leg slowly contracted. She saw a mess of matted feathers on the side of its body and something moving. She bent closer. Maggots. They were moving, curling and uncurling. A hand grabbed her arm.

'Martha' – Auntie Susan hauled her upright – 'you'll get lost if you don't stay with the rest of us.'

'There's a sick bird down there' – Martha pointed – 'behind the big stone.'

'You mustn't wander off on your own.'

'Do something about the bird,' Martha wailed. Susan took a look.

'There's nothing I can do about it, Martha. Birds have to die like everything else.'

'But it's alive. I saw it move.'

'Nonsense. Let me see how many shells you have.' She peered into Martha's paper bag, 'Very good. Come on. I'll help you collect more.' She smiled, patting Martha's head. 'You'd better put your blouse on first, your back's getting burnt.'

'We'll count the shells before tea,' Frank said. David's bag had split and the contents spilled out over the stones. Frank helped him scoop up the shells. Martha handed hers to David. 'I don't have many anyway, you might as well have them.'

'Thanks,' he said, not hesitating to accept them. David was declared the winner. He insisted on sharing the prize, a kite, with Martha by loaning it to her before allowing the other children to fly it.

'Martha must have a go first,' he said, handing her the kite. She watched fascinated as, tail fluttering, it pushed its chest against the wind and curled up into the air.

'It's flying,' she said.

True to her word, Annie waited for the coach to return with the children. 'Well,' she said to Auntie Helen, when she finished polishing the floors, 'I need a cup of tea and a bit of a break before starting home, anyway.'

Hot, tired, red-skinned, sticky children pushed their way through the front door, dragging towels, togs, and paper bags.

'You look like a tomato.' Billy punched Martha playfully on the chest. 'Got anything for me then?'

'No.'

'Come on, come and say good-bye to Annie. I think she's waiting for you. Pet!' he teased.

'You can walk around with me to my bicycle. Can't she?' Annie inquired of Auntie Helen.

'Of course. But don't be too long, it's already late.'

'Well?' Annie looked down and caught Martha's hand as they walked down the corridor towards the front door. 'Why so silent? Didn't you have a grand time?'

'Yes. But . . .'

'Are you not going to tell me?' Annie stopped outside the front door.

'I found a dead bird. I mean, it was alive, I'm sure, but Auntie Susan said it was dead.' A tear slid down Martha's cheek. 'She wouldn't let me keep it. I could have made it better. It was just a little thing.'

'You poor child.' Annie stroked Martha's head, now buried in her skirt. 'It was probably dead already.'

'I saw it move. It had maggots in it.' She was wailing now.

'Well, if it wasn't dead, it will be soon.' She bent down, holding Martha's shoulders. 'Listen to me carefully. It probably fell out of its nest. Did you find it under a tree?'

'No, it was near a wall on the beach.'

'That's it of course. The nest was probably in the wall, and the bird fell out. Just a wee fledgling. Now, it couldn't survive on its own, without its mother or father. It's only kindness to leave it. You could feed it and keep it warm. But you could never teach a fledgling to fly. The only one can do that is another bird that can already fly. If it can't fly, it couldn't protect itself from danger. A bird that can't fly wouldn't be happy. It's better off going to heaven.'

'Birds don't go to heaven.' Billy kicked the door open.

'Don't be horrible, Billy. What would you know about that?' Annie turned towards him, then back to wipe Martha's eyes.

'If it was injured, you should have killed it. Then it wouldn't suffer.' Billy put his hands in his pockets. '*You should have killed it,*' he shouted as he swung round and ran back down the corridor.

8

THIRTEEN-YEAR-OLD Billy slammed the door shut, and leant against it trying to catch his breath, one hand on his chest, the other limply by his side. 'Hawkins is after me.' He slid down against the wall beside the door, pushing his limp hand into his pocket. 'I ran the whole way back from school. I'm goin' to die of exhaustion.'

'You're talkin' rubbish.' Martha, ten now, and grown skinny and tall. 'What you on about?' She turned away from him and walked towards a small table by the window. She sat down. He followed her, and, sitting opposite, glanced back at the door.

'Hawkins hates me, you know.'

'You're dramatizing again.' She turned and looked out of the window, chin in hand. 'You're always teasing him, calling him names. I bet he knows you call him the Hawk. They always find out everything.' She turned to face him.

'Oh shut up. Whose side you on anyway?' He leaned back, arms behind his head, chair swinging. 'You know what? Not only do they find out everything, as you said, but they write it down in your file. They can say what they like. They don't say they don't like you. They report their opinions, and make out that's the truth. Hypocrites.'

The door opened abruptly. Hawkins stared, eyes laser-beaming death at Billy.

'Watts! To your room!' Hawkins shouted, spit spraying. 'Now!' He gratuitously cuffed the lad as Billy attempted to slip by him.

While Frank remonstrated with Billy, Martha made herself scarce, but she was worried, and when she could no longer hear voices coming from the room Billy slept in, she knocked lightly on the door. She opened it sufficiently to see him sitting on the bed, legs drawn up, arms folded and eyes closed.

'You awake?' she whispered.

'Yes.' He turned on to his side and looked towards the door. 'Come in,' he said quietly.

'What happened?' She pushed a sweet into her mouth.

'Nothing really. He went on and on for ages. I didn't listen.' He sat up. 'He's gone to grass me up to Uncle Tony. I think I'm stayin' in here for the rest of the day.' He rolled over and sat up on the bed. 'Shut the door and come over here.' He patted the bed. 'I wouldn't be surprised if they're plotting something pretty nasty for me. Fuckin' bastards.'

'Why is he after you?'

'Oh yeah. I didn't tell you, did I?' He choked with laughter. 'Wait till you hear this.' He rubbed his hands. 'I was kept in for detention. When I'd finished I went to borrow a football from the games cupboard. David said he'd do a bit of practice back here with me.'

'Go on. Hurry up, I don't want to get caught in here.'

'When I went to the gym I heard a noise in the cupboard. I thought, maybe it was a mouse. I don't mind 'em. Anyway, I opened the cupboard door. It was dark, so I didn't notice till I bent down to pick up the ball.'

'What? What?' She was bouncing on the bed.

'Auntie Susan was in there, and so was he.'

'Who?'

'The Hawk.'

'Why? I mean, why were they in the cupboard?'

'They was in a state of undress. Well, not exactly, but his trousers were half off and her skirt. . . He was, you might say, givin' her a biology lesson. A practical.'

'Billy! They can't do it standin' up. They have to lie down. You're makin' it up.'

'No, I'm not. I reckon she's after his money. She's just sellin' herself, if you ask me. What a slag!'

'Don't say that. She's nice to me.' Martha looked down. 'Bitch,' she said under her breath, and looked away from him. 'Do you think she'll leave me?'

'What?' he coaxed, bending towards her until his face was lower than hers and looking up, trying to catch her eye. 'What you mopin' for?'

'Nothing.'

'I'm getting out of here. Tonight. I'm just waiting till it's dark,' he said.

'Where you goin'?'

'I've no bleedin' place to go, have I?' he said.

'We can go to my mum's, if you let me come with you.' She jumped off the bed. 'I got her address. I always keep it in my pocket. Look!' She brought out a crumpled, folded piece of paper and spread it out. 'Here.'

'Even if your mum doesn't mind havin' you back, she won't want me.'

'If she lets me stay, I'll hide you under my bed.' She folded the piece of paper and returned it to her pocket.

'That's a silly idea.' He rummaged in the back of the drawer beside his bed. An avalanche of socks, a book, bits of screwed-up paper, half a chocolate bar, and various

56

other treasures spewed on to the floor. He didn't notice. He was intent on extracting something from the back. He pulled out a note and some change and held out a grubby hand.

'Where did you get that?'

He ignored the question. 'If you want me to, I'll oblige you by stayin' one night at your house. But don't tell anyone, or we'll get nicked.'

An hour later, a small bag of food from tea-time tucked under her arm, inside her cardigan, Martha pushed her coat out of the window of her room, two storeys up. It was a precaution. She would be conspicuous wearing a coat if she was observed leaving. Downstairs, she slipped out of the back door when no one was looking and found the coat. It was raining hard. She watched Billy climbing, sliding, and finally falling the last few feet down the drainpipe from his bedroom window. His hands were black from the dirty pipe and he wiped them on the wet grass. Keeping in the shadow of the hedge, they followed it until they reached the gate. Once outside, the height of the hedge protected them from the eyes of anyone inside.

As usual on a Friday night, Harry was down at the pub. Nancy handed Joe and Mary their week-end pocket money – enough for a trip to the movies and a packet of popcorn each. They knew that Nancy liked to have Friday nights to herself; the tacit agreement was that pocket money was contingent on them taking themselves off for the evening.

When they had left, Nancy took the baby from its pushchair. She washed and dressed it in a hand-knitted blue woollen coat and hat. She put it back into the tattered pushchair which had been Martha's and tucked a blanket around it.

'Are you warm now?' She smiled into its unresponsive face.

Frank went to see Tony, Billy's special uncle at the Home, to tell him that Billy had stolen some money from his jacket pocket. Tony looked puzzled. 'From your pocket?' he said. 'How?'

'I was clearing up the gym, took my jacket off and hung it on the door. It was hot work,' he explained. 'It needed a good clear-out!' He walked towards the door, and stopped when he was pleased with the distance between himself and Tony. He was thinking that no one would believe Billy if he told them about finding Susan and himself in the cupboard. He felt safe about that, but he would feel doubly secure if Tony made a fuss about the stolen money. He was uneasy about the absurd, compromising position he'd been caught in but he wasn't going to allow this mistake to turn into a scandal which might scupper his personal ambitions and therefore his plans for the school.

'I've spoken to the lad.' Frank scratched one ear. 'However, I anticipate your cooperation in this matter; with all your expertise in dealing with delinquent children, I expect you to be more skilled than I in dealing with this kind of problem.' He folded his arms. 'I should hope you will take it very seriously and punish Billy. I've told him I want the money returned voluntarily. The school will not tolerate such behaviour. If a thief is seen to get away with it, it often encourages others to behave the same way.' He unfolded his arms and stuffed his hands into his trouser pockets.

Susan convinced herself that Billy hadn't seen her in the cupboard. Fortunately really, because it might disillusion him, she reasoned. She wondered how Frank would confront the situation. No doubt at all that Billy had seen him. He dashed off after Billy as soon as he could do up his

trousers, without any comment to her, leaving her confused and ashamed in the cupboard. She went back to the
Home and waited for Frank in the staff room. He arrived
later, while she was sipping coffee.

'I'm worried,' she said.

'It's OK. Tony is dealing with Billy.' He poured himself a
coffee and sat down beside her, checking the room and
assuring himself that it was empty.

'What did you say to him?'

'Not much. I told him Billy had taken some cash from my
jacket pocket, and . . .'

'Did he?'

'Yes, of course. He took it as he dashed out. My coat was
hanging on the door. Very smooth, very professional.' He
looked at her and frowned.

'I thought . . . you know . . . it's an impossible situation
for you . . . in the cupboard with me.'

'That isn't a problem. Billy won't even mention it to
Tony. He's smart enough, that child, to know that either no
one would believe him or that in fact it has nothing to do
with his stealing from me. He can hardly trade off the
information against his own mistake, can he?'

'I don't believe in this kind of duplicity. But it's not
something I could discuss with Billy, is it?' She finished her
coffee. 'I'm relieved he didn't recognize me. It's taken away
the obligation to explain it to him; it obviates the necessity
of sticking to my principles of being honest to children.'

'Don't be so bloody worthy, Susan.' Frank got up. 'Billy
took advantage of my lack of trousers to help himself to the
money in my pocket. He's sly. It simply compounds his
guilt.' He patronizingly kissed the top of her head. 'Come
on, I'll take you to the movies.'

Nancy covered the baby's head with another blanket and

59

wheeled it out into the street and on up past the corner shops. She marched swiftly along the pavement for a mile on the way to town, disregarding the rain and looking straight ahead, avoiding eye contact with anyone she might pass. When she reached the first set of traffic lights, she removed the blanket covering the baby's face and continued on into the town. The rain stopped and she lowered the hood on the pushchair and, smiling at the tiny child, she tucked the blankets more securely about it.

Martha and Billy entered the newsagents on the outskirts of the small town. Billy moved towards the shelf displaying comics and, fingering them, appeared interested in a purchase. Martha went straight to the counter to ask the newsagent if he knew the whereabouts of the address on the small piece of crumpled paper she held up to him. He obliged by giving detailed instructions on how to reach her parents' house.

They stared into the windows of the shops as they continued on their adventure. They came to the cinema.

'Let's go to the pictures,' she pleaded.

'No. We can't afford it. In any case, I'm hungry. We'll get food.'

'I brought some with me.' She pulled out a paper bag from inside her coat. 'Here.' She held it up to him. He pulled out a squashed sandwich.

'Thanks,' he said, taking a large bite. 'We don't know when we'll get more supplies.' He returned the rest of the sandwiches.

Nancy watched the children in front of her as they shared something to eat. She could see the lights of the newly built arcade across the street. She was nearly there. Soon she would be sauntering slowly up and down the arcade, looking in at the new fashions and pushing her baby proudly along in the glow of the brightly lit windows. She passed the two children and stopped at the zebra crossing, waiting a second before indicating she was about to cross. The cars stopped.

Martha scrutinized the woman and baby crossing the road with more than usual curiosity. There was something familiar about her. She arrived at the other side of the road and turned towards the arcade. Martha caught her profile.

'Mama!' Martha's arms came up. So focussed on Nancy was she that the car remained unnoticed. Her fragile legs carried her fast across the road. She nearly made it to the other side, but a slow moving car swerved to avoid her unsuccessfully. It brushed her slightly, enough to pitch her onto the pavement. Billy, beyond caring for his own safety, ran after her, wailing. Nancy, surprised by the sudden drama, allowed her normal control over the baby's pushchair to slip. She watched, hands to her face, as it slowly rolled towards the kerb. The baby tipped into the gutter beside Billy, making no sound. The driver, white-faced and defensive, picked up Martha and leant against his car. Some people stared, others came over to sympathize, one picked up Martha's shoe and handed it to the driver, another discreetly called for the emergency services.

Billy could see Martha was moving now, squirming in the driver's arms. He picked up the baby, turned it over and nearly dropped it as he stared into the face of a shiny pink plastic doll.

Nancy snatched it from him, hurriedly shoved it back in its pushchair, brushed off inquiries from by-standers – 'It's okay, not hurt at all, very lucky' – covered it with a blanket, and hurried off home. Billy stood riveted to the pavement until his attention was caught by the arrival of the ambulance and police car making the usual noises. It was clear from Martha's furious tone as she pleaded with the driver to let her go that she wasn't badly hurt. Billy used the confusion to make his getaway.

In the ambulance, despite the gentle questions from the attendant, Martha's rage turned to silence. She refused to answer. At the hospital the further indignity of being undressed and examined, albeit with delicacy, only made her more determined. When the nurse hung Martha's jacket on a hook in an examination room, a folded piece of crumpled paper dropped from the pocket to the floor.

'Now dear,' a voice cooed, as she scrutinized the paper she was busy straightening, 'this must be a clue to who your parents are. This address will tell us something.'

Nancy locked the pushchair in the cupboard under the stairs. Returning to the kitchen she hung her coat to dry near the fire.

The police car, lights on, obliquely angled, parked carelessly in the narrow street.

'Could I come in moment?' the policeman asked, shifting his weight from one foot to the other, sulphur lights casting grotesque shadows on his face.

'What do you want?' Harry, returning from the pub, pushed through the doorway.

'Do you have a ten-year-old daughter?' The policeman scraped his feet on the step as Nancy opened the door wider to let him in.

'Yes.'

The policeman explained that her little girl had had an accident. Nothing serious, you understand. Nancy showed less surprise and shock than the policeman had anticipated; less than he usually saw in relatives of crash victims.

'She doesn't live here,' Nancy shyly told the policeman. 'I'll give you the address of the Council Home.' She searched in her handbag and retrieved a folded piece of paper from a zippered pocket.

'Careless child.' Harry belched, his voice louder than necessary. 'I feel very sorry for the driver. Did she damage the car? Poor bugger.' He sat down heavily. 'Imagine how he must feel.' He shook his head slowly from side to side, staring at the floor. 'That sort of thing can have a terrible effect. It'll probably make a nervous wreck of him.'

'Uncle Tony was okay to me,' Billy told Martha the next day as she sported impressive bandages on a knee and hand. 'You know, that baby in the pushchair was a doll.'

'Don't be daft.'

'I said, it was a doll.'

'The woman was my mother, you know. And she wouldn't push a doll around, now would she? I mean, why would she, eh?'

'I'm tellin' you, it was a doll.'

'You're at it again, Billy Watts. Won't you never stop tellin' fibs?'

'I'm not lying. It's true. You never believe anything I say.' He sat on the bed. 'You know, when you went down on the pavement, I thought you was dead.'

'Oh,' she said, and folded her arms. 'Have you brought me a present?' She leant back against the pillows feeling bruised but important.

'No.'

'Don't you know, Billy, when you visit the sick you have to take them something?'

'Okay.' He put his hand into his back pocket and brought out a folded comic. 'There you are.'

PART TWO

9

Martha sits on the wall, waiting for the bus to take her to work, and, without turning her head, slyly watches the roadsweeper push his great brush along the gutter. Orange peel, beer cans, leaves, and fag-ends succumb.

'What are you staring at?' he asks kindly. He is used to people walking around him, avoiding his brush and cart in an exaggerated way, as if they carried some contagious disease, sometimes turning their heads, rarely catching his eye. He is part of the street furniture.

'Nothing,' she says, remembering that other gutter, the one she encountered when first she entered her own mind's eye. The person who rescued her was like this fellow, with his oilskin uniform. She remembers the feel of the cold, damp, stiff coat against her cheek, as she watches him bend down and scoop up the detritus and toss it expertly into the cart. He turns, and, lifting the handle, pushes the cart towards his next stop. She watches his broad shoulders going away from her and remembers Billy. He'd been proud of the way his exercises had broadened his physique, and she thinks of the last time she saw him, three years ago, when he left the Home at the age of sixteen. He just walked off. He didn't turn back and wave and she hadn't seen him since. Now she is sixteen and it is her turn to explore the world above the gutter.

She jumps down from the wall as she sees the bus lumbering to the stop. The roadsweeper stops, turns towards the bus, watches as she steps onto it, leans with one hand on the broomhandle, and waves with the other. She returns his wave, pays her fare, goes up the stairs, and settles into a front seat. She has a job washing up in a café, and digs with a Mrs Wall, who provides bed and breakfast. The most exciting aspect of her new life is having a friend, Lisa, who works with her in the café. She doesn't know Martha comes from a Children's Home. She figures she might be seen as a freak if she is found out, if it is discovered she was so unfit and unlovely a child that her parents abandoned her. Here she is on the edge of a new beginning and she isn't going to have it messed up by carrying old burdens. Lisa appears to her to be in control of everything that happens to her. She will take a few tips from Lisa. The bus reaches her stop and Martha walks the few paces to the café early enough for Lisa and her to chat before they open the shop.

'You all right in there?' Lisa taps on the toilet door, where Martha is attempting to inhale something that couldn't taste worse if it were a boxer's jockstrap.

'Whoa, fine thanks,' she manages to say.

'You sound as if you're choking.'

'No, no, I'm okay.' How could anyone enjoy this stuff, she thinks. Another of life's interminable mysteries, riddles, and enigmas to be solved. Another is Dick, the manager of the café, who during the few days she has been working finds excuses to touch her, and passes through the narrow entrance to the counter when she slips through too often to be a coincidence. She doesn't want to offend him by suggesting he is becoming too familiar in case she has misinterpreted the way he presses against her. Besides, he's the boss. She throws the cigarette butt between her legs into the lavatory and pulls the chain. She must talk to Lisa about Dick.

'You're not afraid of anyone, are you?' Martha twists the cloth around the inside of a glass. 'The way you treat Dick, I mean, you don't seem to worry what he thinks of you.'

'Why should I? I don't know why you are so timid with him. If he touched me uninvited I'd throw him over my shoulder. He knows, so wouldn't even try.' She draws a cup of coffee from the urn and flaps her hands at the steam.

'How do you know he isn't being friendly? He said it to me when I pulled away from him.'

'God, you are naïve. It's out of place in the circumstances. He's the boss so thinks he can go around groping the more innocent girls on the staff.' She wipes the counter top, moves the salt, pepper, and tomato sauce bottles, and lines them up with the vinegar. 'Look, there's a customer, go and see what she wants.' She tosses the damp cloth into the sink. 'We'll talk later, okay? After work, in the pub, yes?'

'Thanks.' Martha picks up her pad and ballpoint and moves towards the table.

Later the same day and not far away, Billy pushes home the bolt he has fixed on to the door of his room and strips off to his underpants. He scrutinizes the picture of Perfect Man pasted above the mirror. Superman. He's seen all the movies. He'd give anything to be able to fly. Not with a cape, of course, that's just kid's stuff. He wouldn't mind flying a superfast jet, but he knows that to join the Air Force you need more education than he's ever likely to have. On the other hand he could join the paratroopers, as he knows their entry standards are not so high because someone else from his school joined the paras and they weren't full of brains.

He unwraps the parcel he has secreted under his coat and examines his purchase. A piece of printed paper with line drawings and instructions flutters to the ground when he pulls out the chest expander. He plants his feet half a yard apart and, grasping the expander with both hands, heaves. Nothing happens.

'Blimey,' he says. Just needs running-in, he reasons, and, placing one end on a foot, attempts to loosen it. It gives a little. He takes off one of the metal springs, before flexing it with a foot and both hands. It moves. Now for the big test. A few deep breaths and he yanks it with both hands, leaning with his back arched, until it is completely extended across his chest.

'Jesus bloody Christ,' he shrieks as the thing shoots from his hands, straining his arms, and nipping at his skin as it takes in the scant tufts of prized nineteen-year-old chest hairs. It clings to him for a few seconds like a clawing, crazed wild cat before he pulls it away and throws it onto the bed. 'Right,' he says to no one, 'I'll bleedin' get you.'

He hurriedly dresses, checks the change in his pocket, and takes out a small note book. 'Four more lucky people tonight,' he mutters to himself as he checks down the list in the book before leaving his room and slipping out into the early evening. There are two telephone boxes in Western Street he hasn't used before. He'd noticed them on his way home.

When Martha left the Council Home, Auntie Susan had checked that she had her mother's address and telephone number. Her feelings towards her mother, tangled and secret as they were, had become clearer in one direction since being out and alone. There were practicalities like being short of money and days still to go before pay-day.

On each of the nights since she left the Home she has telephoned her mother. Every time the telephone was answered the other end, she'd been too apprehensive to speak. On her way to meet Lisa she turns back after passing the coin boxes and dials the number again.

'Hello,' a man's voice answers, interrupted by the mechanical hiccup of the coin. 'Hello,' he repeats.

A croaking noise which forces its way from Martha's mouth is an improvement on the previous silence.

'Fuck off.' She nearly drops the handpiece at the reply. 'Bugger off, whoever you are.' The voice at the other end is not very encouraging. 'If you're looking for herself, you won't have any luck, mate. Anonymous faggot.' The voice drifts away as if talking to someone else. Martha replaces the receiver. She waits ten minutes before dialling again.

'Hello.' A woman's voice answers this time.

'Hello.' Martha surprises herself.

'Who's that? Hello, hello.'

'It's Martha here.' Silence the other end.

'Hello,' Martha says again.

'Martha, er . . . Eagan?'

'Yes, Mother.'

'How are you?'

'I'm all right, thank you, Mother. I'm okay, that is, I'm out now. You know, living in a room, er, in a boarding-house near you. Out of the Home.'

'What's it like?'

'It's all right.' Martha tries to laugh. 'I'd like to see you.' She pulls a face at the telephone. 'I mean, could you meet me somewhere?'

'When?'

71

'Could we meet to-night? It's very important.'

Nancy sighs. 'Yes,' she says, 'of course I can meet you. But I can't do much to help you, you know. You better understand that.'

'Can you meet me in the White Hart? You know where it is? In an hour? I'd better go now, there's someone waiting to use the phone.' Martha is aware of a moving figure impatiently waiting outside.

'Yes. I'll be there. You're too young to drink in pubs, Martha. I don't like going into a pub on my own, so don't be late.' The pips are going so Martha inserts another coin.

The person waiting is pacing around the telephone box, stopping now to press his face grotesquely against the glass. 'I'll be wearing a red coat.'

'I don't know why you're telling me that.' Nancy is impatient. 'See you in an hour, then.'

'Mother.' Martha's voice is suddenly childish. 'I'm looking forward to seeing you.' She puts the telephone back in the cradle before picking it up again. The cord nearly tears her hand as she pulls it away, disconnecting the handpiece from the rest.

'Thanks very much.' The door swings open and a hand grasps the handpiece. With the other hand dialling 999, Billy holds the dead handpiece to his head and grins in recognition as he says to the empty instrument, 'Yes, officer, get down here fast. There's a vandal just wrecked the telephone and ruined my evening's fun.' He dances out into the road still holding the handpiece.

'Billy Watts! Where did you spring from?' Martha is laughing as she follows him into the street.

'Here,' he says, as he presses it into the hand of a passing stranger. 'Here, there's a phone call for you.' He grabs Martha's hand. 'Leg it,' he says, and they head down the road.

Lisa sits with her legs crossed, on a stool at the bar of the Oranges and Lemons. She's come in to look for a flat. A room would do. She hasn't got long to fix it up. Martha will be arriving in an hour and that could mess up her patch. Trouble is, there aren't usually many punters around this early in the evening. She doesn't like the look of any of them here so far. She's never had a place of her own. Too much trouble. She exists, as long as she feels comfortable, in whatever place she can land herself without being too pushy. So long as there is food and shelter she isn't too fussy about who shares the bed. She wouldn't tolerate bullying or any kind of violence and she wouldn't take any lip either. She has her standards.

'You're early,' she says as Martha and Billy arrive out of breath. 'Aren't you going to introduce me?' She eyes Billy as he says his name. 'Excuse me a moment, will you, I have to go and freshen my lippy,' she says, and moves towards the Ladies.

'Listen you, Billy Watts, I forgot about her. She doesn't know I come from a Council Home and I don't want you telling her.' Martha takes his arm. 'Promise?'

'I don't see why it bothers you.'

'People think there must be something wrong with you, or that you've done something dreadful, if they find out where you've come from.'

'Rubbish. What do you want to drink? I'm buying. I just got out.'

'Where?'

'The nick.' He grins as the barman pretends not to hear. 'You could say this is my comin'-out party.'

'What did you do?'

'I'll tell you later.' He nudges her towards a table as Lisa returns with her lips freshly painted.

'Another of your stories, Billy.' They sit down.

'No, honest. I'm livin' at the Bail Hostel, just up the road.' Lisa's accommodation hopes fade at the news. Pity. She likes the look of Billy.

'We'll have a couple of drinks here and then I'll take you down the club. So what are you havin'?'

Billy says to Lisa, a few drinks later, on the way to the club: 'Hold onto her while I make an urgent phone call.' He leans her against the railings by the public telephone. Lisa clutches Martha's arm to prevent her slipping sideways. Her legs are playing tricks on her.

'Me mother's probably been picked up by some bloke by now,' Martha wails.

'Shut up, you silly cow. You'd get picked up an' all if it wasn't for me. Three drinks and you're anybody's,' he sneers.

He keeps the telephone door open with his foot as he dials, and slips the coin home. No answer. 'Fuck!' he says, and works his finger down the next number on his list and dials again.

'Hello.'

'Mrs Watts, is it?'

'Miss Watts.'

'Someone calling himself your husband asked me to ring you. I wonder who it can be? A friend of yours?'

'Who's that?' The voice is irate.

'Your secret is safe with me.' It doesn't sound like Billy. Years of mimicking Authority is coming in useful.

'You are in a lot of trouble, Miss Watts.'

'Who are you?'

'I'm your long-lost son, Miss Watts. Lost, but not gone forever, you might say.'

'I don't have a son.'

'That's what you tell everybody, isn't it? But I know different.'

'But I haven't . . .'

'Did you think you could rid yourself of me so easily, eh?'

'Who are you?'

'It isn't surprising you don't know me, Mother, after all it's been nineteen years since you threw me away. Do you know they used to beat me every day till my skin burst and bled.' His fist is working, clenching and unclenching.

'Go away.' This is a good one. They didn't usually hold the conversation for this length of time. Billy's lucky day.

'I'm going to give you a chance, Mother.'

'I'm not your mother.'

'I said, I'll give you another chance. But we'll have to start from the beginning. I'll have to come out again.' His free hand is in his pocket, working away, pulling at himself. 'And to come out, I'll have to get in, won't I, eh? Born-again Billy!' There is a gulping sound at the other end of the phone. 'You'll breast-feed me, too, Mother, won't you?' he screams at the phone as it is slammed down, but not before his efforts draw a sigh of relief.

They pass the White Hart on the way to the club. Martha steadies herself against the wall outside and peers through the large plate-glass window into the smokey interior of the bar. In the far corner she sees a woman sitting on her own. The woman's mouth opens. She is looking at Martha.

'Look, Billy, there's me mother.' She pulls him around to see.

'Where?'

'There! She's lookin' at me.' The woman raises her arm, her mouth still open. 'She's calling me.'

'Don't be daft,' he says, kicking a cigarette packet into the gutter. 'It's not your mother; it's just some woman orderin' a drink.'

10

FRANK HAWKINS TOSSES the car keys in the air as he walks from his car into the public bar. Two doubles are enough to dull his senses. Doubles or couples, it is all the same. What secret does everyone share that is denied to him? There have been many women since Susan, but no single one gave him what he needed. He visits his women friends in rotation, keeping them interested but not too close. He remembers his uncle's collection of old clocks. He'd wind them in turn to keep them working. It always fascinated the boy Frank, the care his uncle took over his precious clocks. Considering the care with which he nurtures his women friends' interest in him, he is disappointed by his failure tonight. He has mishandled his plans, anticipated incorrectly who is available, finds himself alone at the end of his day.

It isn't raining any more. He will go for a walk along the canal before returning to his flat. There is nothing personal about his flat except a faint smell of himself. Moderately tidy, newly painted in a dull combination suitable for a teacher on the way up, nothing notably arresting or controversial about his selection of books, not too many with 'Marxist' in the title, and no sexual manuals or girlie magazines. Smutty mags are in the desk, third drawer down, at the back. The atmosphere of the room is bland and cold, except for one small area which sings with colour. He holds this sight in his mind's eye as he reluctantly leaves the warmth and noise of the bar.

He begins his journey back to his flat and thinks about the one welcome aspect, his beloved begonias. Through a glass door, leading from his living-room, on what was once the roof of the bathroom of the flat below, he has erected a small but charming conservatory. It is full of a collection in which he takes great pride, nurturing each plant tenderly to produce glorious, healthy blooms. He will come home from a stressful day at school, kick off his shoes, and walk barefoot into the warmth and colour of this special place. He has placed blinds inside the glass to protect his precious plants from too much sun.

Tonight he will calm himself with a bit of propagation. He will clean his scalpel with methylated spirit and carefully slice through the medium rib and main veins of the fleshy leaves and marvel at their fecundity. One leaf can produce a dozen new baby plants. He pictures them. The leaves are almost as variable as the hypnotic blooms: maroon, silver, red, green, mahogany leaves, some spotted, others hairy. Short, tall, trailing and rambling and variegated blooms, some with edges painted with contrasting colours. He loves his 'Venus', nipple-pink and delicate, the milky-white 'Snow-bird', and the lovely 'Can-Can', a large, welcoming cave with a lush red centre. He thinks of dreamy 'Full-moon', creamy and enticing, and 'Yellow Melody', with her clusters of small, pure flowers, sun-coloured and dainty.

He walks along the canal bank to clear his head. The fresh air will prevent a hangover. He has made the mistake in the past of facing a classroom of children hungover, and it wasn't a pretty sight. Someone is tap-tapping behind him, as he walks down the tow-path. It sounds like a solitary someone wearing stiletto heels. A low-hanging branch catches his head, showering him with drops of water. He welcomes the coolness. The tapping continues. He turns abruptly around. No one there. The noise is coming from an area around a bush, beside a park bench. He walks towards the sound.

In the light of a street lamp he can make out something small moving under the bench; it is a bird. A bird? At night? How strange, he thinks, as he bends down to examine it more easily. It has a snail in its mouth and is smashing it against the path, attempting to break the shell. It fixes an eye on Frank before scurrying into the interior of the bush.

He is disturbed by this encounter and muses over it as he returns to his car. He knows the children call him 'Hawk'. It distresses him to recognize that he frightens them, and whispered staff room talk enraged him when he discovered his unwelcome nickname. He loathes the staff for their disloyalty in picking it up from the children. Hawk. Predator. Bird of Prey. Did he earn this predatory reputation? Was it justified, he wondered? He can feel the tension corroding him, wearing out the old engine, encrusting him with bad humour.

Mrs Wall is generous with her stories of the disparate characters who people her lodging-house. She embellishes whatever tenuous attributes she sees in them, inventing tales from small occurrences, entertaining her friends and tenants with past adventures. She sits, legs akimbo, in a red satin dressing-gown at the breakfast table, openly directing the conversation towards her favourite lodger. She can feel a cool breeze between her legs, from the open door.

'What do you think will happen now that the Prime Minister is so unpopular, er, according to the latest opinion polls, that is?' She doesn't wait for an answer, rattling the cups she passes to her tenants. She enjoys playing the matriarch at breakfast, handing morsels to her favourites. She's brightest in the mornings. 'A little more marmalade? It's lime flavoured.' She opens her legs and her robe slips away from them unseen by her guest. 'Here' – she scoops a spoonful of the marmalade on to Mr Harris's plate – 'very tasty,' she says. 'Some more toast? You're looking peaky today, Martha, isn't she, everyone?' – turning round, lizard eyes darting from one lodger to another, checking the audience interest. She's a star and no mistake.

'We're a bit late this morning, aren't we?' she says to Hilda, who lives with her little boy in the room above Martha. She closes her legs and puts her hand under the table, wraps the robe around her, and pulls the child onto her lap.

'Timmy woke late,' says Hilda, looking at the clock, and then bends across to Timmy to hand him some milk.

'Had a restless night, did he?' Mrs Wall pushes a cup of tea towards her. 'Help yourself to toast, Hilda.' She points to it. 'It could mean a General Election.' She looks around again for some response. 'My son,' she says with emphasis, arms around Timmy, holding her hands together in a prayer-like fashion, 'my son says it's inevitable given the economic situation in this country. Another election will give more strength to the Prime Minister if there is a larger majority. It's not that the government is making mistakes, going in the wrong direction, it's not that the economic policy isn't right on target, it's that they need a stronger hand to push it all the way.'

She pauses, looks around again to detect who is listening.

'Don't you think so, Mr Harris? Another term of office and they'll prove successful?' She takes a tea-towel and wipes Timmy's face as he lets his milk dribble down his chin. 'Don't mind me, Hilda, here . . .' She hands the tea-towel and child to his mother. 'My son says they need the larger majority to give them muscle and courage to enforce the correct policies at home.' Martha and Hilda both get up from the table. 'My son, he doesn't agree with the government, but he says they know what they are doing.'

'Well, well,' says Mr Harris, poking at the butter. 'I wonder if it's going to rain today. Should I take my umbrella, do you think?'

Martha leaves the house as Hilda pushes her little boy out in his pushchair. Mrs Wall doesn't like them staying in all day in case the child disturbs the other tenants. Timmy is two years old. Sometimes his mother slaps him when he won't stop crying. She isn't nasty to him all the time. When she talks to him she looks into his face as if it is the most beautiful thing she has ever seen. His mother takes him down to the park most days, if it isn't raining.

Martha watches them as she waits at the bus stop. When they get to the park the mother will let the little boy out of his pushchair to run around. She can't run. She can only walk, using the pushchair to balance herself. One leg is shorter than the other and both are stiff. Martha is fascinated by her rhythmic lurch as she swings from side to side pushing her child. One foot skips as she lifts the other. How will she balance when the child is too old to squash into the pushchair? Thinks Martha: I bet she just lives for him.

'I'll let you have some cash if you're a bit short.' Billy's hand is in his pocket. 'Here, how much do you want?'

'Where did you get that?' Martha looks at the roll of notes in his fist.

'Never mind.' He hands her three. 'Let me know when you need more.'

'I'll pay it back.' She pushes the money into her purse.

'Why bother?' He takes her hand. 'C'mon, come and have some coffee.'

'Where did you get it from, Billy?'

'I said, never mind, okay?'

Billy has a nice little line going for him. He does business in clubs and pubs and supplies any variety of drug in small quantities. A dealer. A dealer in happiness, he tells himself. Doin' a bit of good. Never takes the stuff himself. He gets invited to some exotic parties. And he always has the readies. Quite the philanthropist, helping Martha out sometimes, at the same time as sending a small dart of bliss into anyone ignorant enough to trade with him. A sort of social worker, really. It pays for his telephone calls too, and his work-outs at the local gym.

'Wait for me here a minute,' he says, placing a cup of coffee in front of her. 'I have to make an urgent telephone call.'

'Hello.'

'Hello, Mr Watts?'

'Yes, hello.'

'Sitting comfortably, are you?' Billy is sweating.

'Yes, who's that?'

'Your son.'

'My what?'

'Your son.'

'What?'

'I said, it's your son.'

'Don't be ridiculous' – a nervous laugh – 'Who are you?' The voice is commuter-belt style; loaded, thinks Billy. 'I don't have a son.'

'Well, you do now. And furthermore you have had one for twenty years. Didn't Shirley tell you?'

'Shirley? Who's Shirley?'

'My mother, stupid.'

'Don't call me stupid. I think you must have the wrong number. There's been a mistake.'

'I'm the mistake. I'm your mistake. You made a mistake when you fucked Shirl and went off leaving her expecting a little bastard.'

'Ugh!' This one is too good to be true: Billy hasn't had a success like this for months.

'What are you going to do about it, eh? About me, your son?'

'Well, actually, I don't know. I mean I don't remember anyone called Shirley.' Billy puts a coin into the telephone.

'Don't remember her. Too bad. She has had a little reminder of you around for all these years.' Billy laughs. 'What are you going to do for me then?'

'What do you want?'

'What do you think?'

'Money, I suppose. You're blackmailing me, aren't you?'

'Now, that had never crossed my mind. What I really wanted was just to meet you. To meet my own dear daddy. Just to see your face, to know you, to find out what you're really like. I've carried a mental picture of you all these years.' Billy sniffs, blows his nose. 'I've missed you, missed a father's love.' His voice is broken. *'Dad!'*

'Jesus, stop!' There is a pause. 'Just tell me what to do,' the voice says softly. 'What can I do to help?'

'Meet me in half an hour at the town centre, under the clock. And then we can talk and get to know each other properly,' Billy croaks.

'Okay. How shall I know you?'

'Don't worry, you'll know me. Look for a young man of

twenty wearing an off-white jacket, red shirt and green tie and carrying a white stick. I'll be there.'

'A white stick?'

'Yes, I'm blind. My mother beat me up. Blinded me.' He hesitates, coughs. 'I'll give you all the details when I see you.'

'Oh. Oh my God! How terrible. I'll be there.'

'Don't keep me waiting too long. I'm afraid of traffic, you know, me being blind, it makes me nervous of being run down.'

'Yes, yes, of course. Er . . . what's your name?'

'Billy, Billy Watts,' he says as he replaces the receiver. 'I've got your number,' he murmurs under his breath.

11

'EVEN IF YOU found your parents through your telephone calls, you will have ruined any chance you might have with them by your hostility.' Martha watches Billy hunched over his coffee, quietly laughing. They are having a snack before meeting Lisa in the pub. 'I don't think you care if you find them or not, right?'

'Why don't you shut up?' He's rocking on his chair. 'It's all right for you, you know who yours are.'

'Possibly. I'm not sure the story I have is true. I can't say I believe it.'

'Why?'

'Well, you know the story they tell, the one Susan told me about Harry dumping me on the doorstep, Nancy goin' mad in hospital and our neighbour seeing the bit in the newspaper about the abandoned baby and Nancy claimin' it was her child, me?'

'Yes, of course, you've told me before. What's new?'

'Well, I don't believe it. It is my opinion, and I have a feelin' I'm right' – she folds her arms and leans back – 'that Harry dropped me in the nearest river and not on the doorstep, and that he only agreed to Nancy claiming the baby found on the doorstep as a convenience in case the body of the other baby was found.'

'Eh? Wait a minute.' Billy looks puzzled, picking at his nails, looking at them thoughtfully. 'If they dropped you in the river you wouldn't be here.'

'Well, they dropped their child, is what I mean. I'm the one found on the doorstep, left there by someone unknown.'

'So you don't know who you are?'

'No.'

'Do you believe that?'

'No. Well, about as much as I believe their story.' She shakes her head. 'I haven't any conclusive evidence.'

'You haven't any evidence at all, have you?'

'No.' She laughs. 'Get us another coffee, okay?'

'Okay. You do have some funny ideas, Martha.'

'It's not much of a story, is it? I mean there's more to it than I've told you.'

'All right then.' He gets up. 'Tell me the rest when I get back.'

Meanwhile a certain Mr Watts is looking for a young man with an off-white jacket, red shirt, green tie, and a white stick.

'Go ahead, give us another thrilling bit of your history then.' Billy spills some as he settles another coffee on to the table.

'Perhaps that funny woman – Edith, her name was, I vaguely remember her – perhaps she gave birth to me and, trying to hide it from her husband, said she found me on her doorstep. She was very odd, Billy. Used to look at me in a most peculiar way, sort of side-ways, keeping her head turned slightly away from me. She said she found me on her doorstep; she told me when she came to visit me once – on my birthday, I think it was.'

'You're making it up.'

'No, no. It's true.'

'You're always talking about yourself. Very preoccupied with yourself, you are.' Martha turns from him. 'Come here,' he says, 'come here,' and he shifts his chair towards her. 'Come here, Martha.' She can feel his warm breath on her face. 'What about me?'

'Billy,' she says uneasily, 'leave off,' and she turns away from him again. 'What about Lisa, eh?' she begins to stand up. 'She's waiting for us.'

'She'll be all right. We can find her later if she's still around, hasn't picked up anyone.'

Frank sits in the bar remembering, with distaste, this morning's school assembly. Yesterday the Head had explained to the pupils how standards of dress in the school were dropping. Some of the children sniggered. He was concerned, he said, that many pupils were not wearing the obligatory school uniform, the boys dressing in a slovenly way, without school ties, and the girls not behaving in a very lady-like manner. This had to stop. He wanted them to start the new term well, and asked the boys to remember their ties the next day, and asked the girls to remember that they represented the school and its reputation and to take pride in their appearance.

This morning the boys had brought in their ties and the girls had put them on. The Head ignored them. In the staff room at first morning break, teachers were divided. Some thought the Head should have made it a show of strength; others thought ignoring them showed the right level of contempt. One teacher, Mrs Kelly, thought the kids were right, that the Head had been wrong to put the emphasis on appearance when there were so many other important issues left unmentioned.

'I suspect the girls persuaded the boys to give them their ties,' suggested Frank, and watched for a response.

'I've something you should read.' Mrs Kelly is sorting through her bag and pulls out a book. 'This should be required reading for all teachers,' she says, handing it to Frank. It is *Educating Adolescent Girls*, by Eileen Chandler.

'Thanks.' Frank takes the book. 'I'll have a look at it later.' He tucks it under one arm and takes a sip of coffee. 'I'm surprised you have time to read anything with a heavy teaching programme and your household duties to perform.' He bows slightly, smiling at her. But Mrs Kelly is not amused.

'You're impossible,' she says.

Now he is contemplating the responsibility involved in management of the school. It is difficult enough being a teacher without taking on further administrative responsibilities. He is already, like many other teachers at the school, worried about whom to support in industrial action. On the one hand you have the problem of fair pay and conditions, and you have to look after yourself, and on the other there's the pupils to consider. Last year one of the 'O' level biology classes had no proper teacher for the whole course. They existed throughout on supply teachers, which was most unsatisfactory, and resulted in a poor showing in exams. He knows of one teacher in the school who sends his own child to a private school. And if the money is cut off any further he thinks he'll hear of others following this example.

He realizes that if he applies for the job of Deputy Head, as is his intention, then these conundrums will come more sharply into focus for him and he'll have to take one side or the other, and be seen to do so. There will be no avoiding the choice. He has come into the bar to relax and take his mind off these daily problems.

Lisa stares at him for a few seconds and then gives him what she considers a provocative smile. She is sitting at the bar next to Frank Hawkins, though she doesn't know the connection between him and Billy and Martha. He takes out a cigarette case, opens it, and holds it towards her. 'My name is Frank,' he says. 'Won't you have one of these?'

'Ta very much.' She takes one. 'I'm Lisa.' She picks up her glass, drains it, and places it near him on the bar.

'I'll have a large one. Bell's,' she says. 'Ice and water, thanks.' Her accent adapts to his. She is an expert at verbal camouflage. 'Very smart cigarette case.' She nods towards it.

'Yes, isn't it? It's an antique.' Frank picks it up from the bar and pushes it into his pocket. 'Shall we sit in the corner?'

'No. I'll stay here if you don't mind.'

Fast worker, she thinks, trying to get in a cosy position too rapidly for her comfort. 'What do you do?' she says, throwing the emphasis on to him, playing for time.

'I'm a teacher.' He puts the glasses down again on the bar and settles himself back on the stool. 'School teacher.'

'I've always fancied myself as a teacher.' She looks at herself in the mirror behind the bar.

'You should follow your ambition then, Lisa.' He smiles at her. 'I should say, looking at you' – he examines her face as she turns towards him – 'that you're not too long out of school yourself.'

'I would have thought it an avantage to be nearer in age to the children, the better to understand them.' She notes the hair below his clean white cuffs, the way it bunches there before thinning out across his hands, the light catching it glinting blond. 'I'm bored with this conversation.' She gulps down the remainder of the whisky. 'Couldn't we talk about something more exciting?'

'Would you prefer a philosophical discussion? A dialectic

on the meaning or absence of meaning of life. Something along those lines, eh? I put in a lot of time considering that one. It's a big conundrum for me; perhaps you can enlighten me,' he sneers.

'Blimey,' she says, 'what makes you think you can sort that lot out? You'll drive yourself crazy.' She pushes her glass in his direction again. 'I thought we could talk about something like, what was the worst thing you've ever done, for instance?' She notices Billy and Martha push through the door to the bar. 'Something really evil?' She nudges him, grinning, as the others come over to the bar. 'Let me introduce my friends before you start.' She turns and sees a look of recognition pass between Billy and Frank.

'You want to be careful of him, Lisa.' Billy is delighted to be on neutral territory and of equal status with Frank. What a chance. He mustn't throw away the opportunity to get his own back, to even the score. 'Did he give you that old one about being a teacher, Lisa?' Billy stares at Frank. 'He's a laboratory assistant really. Works at the clap clinic. Helps people jerk off.' He turns to Lisa. 'Enjoys his work. But his hands are full of germs, Lisa, so don't let him grope you. You never know what you might catch.'

'You know all about that place, of course, Billy. One of the clinic's better customers, I believe,' says Frank.

'Hello,' says Martha, as Frank turns towards her, still laughing.

'Well, hello, Martha, what a nice surprise.' He looks at her closely. 'It is Martha, isn't it?'

'Yes.'

'Why don't you all join me and tell me how you are and what has been happening to you, over a nice meal?' His arms are paternally guiding them. 'We can catch up with each other's news. Unless you'd like a drink first?' He winks at Billy. 'My treat,' he says. 'I know how tricky it can be when you're young and haven't much cash.' He turns towards Lisa. 'You must come too,' he says. 'We can't leave you here on your own, can we?' He turns to the others for assent.

'Ta,' says Billy, happy to take advantage of Frank's generosity. He considers how different his attitude is now that he is no longer his teacher, and he, Billy, is no longer in his grasp. He'll never forgive Frank, wouldn't forgive anyone. It's too dangerous. After all, people just repeat the same things, don't they? He wouldn't trust anyone to change their ways. Frank was bad to Billy: though other people might not think grassing up a kid was serious, Billy did. He remembered the way his heart pounded as he ran to find Martha all those years ago when he was thirteen.

12

'YOU KNOWN BILLY a long time, then?' Lisa moves towards the door of the café to lock it now they are closed.

'Yeah. We were at school together.' Martha takes two cups from the stack.

'He's much older than you, isn't he?'

'Three years. We knew each other anyway.' She fills the cups with tea from the urn, places them in the saucers, and takes them over to a table by the window.

'Strange. People don't usually know kids in their school unless they're in the same year.' She pulls down the blind and clicks it in place on the door.

'Well, we did. Anyway, it's boring. Come and have your tea.' She places the cups exactly opposite each other, and sits down and sips.

'He's nice looking.' Lisa sits down.

'Who?'

'Billy.'

'I never noticed.'

'C'mon, who you kidding? You spend enough time together.' She laughs. 'Aren't you going out?'

'No, it isn't like that. We've just known each other a long time, you know, like brother and sister.'

'You should hang on to him.' She studies Martha's face. 'If you have a scene with someone you like and know like Billy, you don't have the problem of squandering your time on someone you've no real affection for.' She pauses. 'I've watched the way he looks at you. He's really fond of you,' she says as if it's a gift.

'I've never had a boyfriend.'

'You haven't any experience?'

'None.'

'I have. If you get together with a bloke who knows you well they don't expect you to be someone you ain't. There's blokes who want to make you their ideal girl. They find someone they hardly know who they fantasize about. Then they start adjusting your make-up and dress, trying to influence what you say and do. It's their idea of romance.'

'Does it matter?'

''Course it does. You've got to be what they want you to be, or you've betrayed them, let them down. Funny, isn't it? I don't know why those sort don't stick to those rubber dolls they find in sex shops.'

'Eh? What do you mean? Tell me.' Martha is giggling, the realization emerging against her will, like toothpaste from a tube with the cap still on. 'No, don't,' she says, 'I don't think I want to know.' There is a tap at the door.

'Ignore the creep,' Lisa says, seeing Martha rise. 'Whoever it is can fuck off, we're going home.' They don't bother to investigate and can't see that it is Frank outside the steamed-up window. But he is persistent, and when he doesn't succeed in persuading anyone to open the door he waits in the doorway of a newsagent across the road to watch them leave.

Dropping down the steps two at a time, he keeps Lisa in

view as he follows twenty yards behind. The arcade is behind him now, and he notices that the last shop they pass is an off-licence. She turns into a small street, tapping on her heels, hugging her coat tightly against the wind; she stops ten yards along the street. She is taking something out of her bag. He remains watching at the end of the street. Now she is turning the key in a door. It is quite dark; the street lights throw the doorway into shadow. She enters the house and shuts the door. He walks closer to the house and notices a light go on in an upstairs room. Scrutinizing the three doorbells he reckons it must be the top bell for the top room as there are no other lights on except the hallway. He fishes in his pocket to check he has enough money and walks swiftly back to the off-licence, figuring she will probably change after work. Better give her a little longer to get herself ready for him. Returning, he perches on a wall opposite her house, the better to observe any visitors she might have and to see if she leaves for an evening's entertainment.

He rings the bell. She takes her time answering and he wonders if she went straight out while he was getting the booze. Just his luck, he thinks.

'What do you want?' She isn't friendly. 'And how did you know where I live? She keeps her hand on the slightly open door.

'Can I come in?' He smiles and produces the tissue-wrapped bottle from his pocket. 'Thought we might have a drink together.' He steps into the hallway and nods in the direction of the stairs. 'In your room.'

'I suppose so. It isn't my room. I'm only staying the week.'

'Who does it belong to?'

'Never mind.' She begins to climb the stairs. 'Come up anyway.'

'You are a very attractive young lady.' Frank is seated on the chair opposite the bed and pulling the cork from the bottle.

'I'm not blind,' she says. 'I can see in the mirror.' She takes out a cigarette, the last in the pack. Frank places the bottle on the floor and fumbles in his pocket,

'Have one of these.' He pushes the packet towards her.

'Ta,' she says and leans forward to catch the light.

The balls drop with a satisfying thud and trundle along to the opening. Billy places the triangle on the pool table. 'Sit there' – he nods towards a stool near one side of the table – 'up against the wall, so you won't get in the way.' He picks up the stool and places it where he wants it. Martha perches, one foot curled around the stool leg, the other on the floor. She isn't interested in playing pool, so he's challenged one of the blokes who used to work on the site with him. He picks up the black ball and places it on the spot, and then stares steadily at her for a few seconds. 'You comfortable?'

'Yes.'

'Good.' He arranges the other balls in the triangle and takes the white one and rubs it against his trouser groin as if he's about to bowl. It is warm and noisy in the bar. He ignores the crush of people crowding the table, and sets it down in the semi-circle. He picks up the chalk and works it around the end of the cue, looks up at her again. 'You want a drink?'

'Please.'

'Okay.' He places the cue against the wall beside her. 'Back in a minute.'

'C'mon, mate, stop wasting time.' His opponent is impatient to start.

'You shut up,' says Billy. 'I'm only gettin' her a drink

while she watches us.' He pushes through the crowd. When he returns he places another few coins on the edge of the table in order to indicate he will play another game when they've finished this one, and then hands Martha her drink.

'Toss.' Billy hands his friend a coin.

It will be Billy to break. He looks towards Martha and keeps his eyes steadily on hers for a full minute. Then he takes the cue, bends over the table, and makes a good break, the balls well distributed and splayed out: one slips briskly into the pocket. He walks over to her before taking his second shot, stands close enough to feel her body warmth, leans his head down until his chin is on her shoulder. 'We've been goin' around for ages, Martha.' He looks into her face briefly before slipping around to the other side of the table to line up the shot, bending over, assessing the angles. He moves past her, catching her eyes again, taking the shot from the other end. Another good one, his turn again. He uses the need to deliberate over the shot yet again to brush past her, hesitating in front of her to press himself gently against her body. He sighs heavily before leaving for the other end of the table, working the cue into the dent in the chalk and lining up the next shot, which leaves his opponent to play.

The noise in the bar is sufficient to prevent anything he says from being overheard. 'A man, you know, well, he needs more than you give me.' He's grinning and looking at her mouth. She can feel and smell his breath.

'You're the best friend anyone ever had, Billy.' Her cheeks flush hot; she is experiencing an exhilarating feeling she's never had before.

'It's more than *that* I feel for you.' He nuzzles her neck, his hair against her face, spreading the sensation all over her body.

'Ah Billy.' Words quiver on the edge of her breath. 'Let's get out of here,' she hears herself whisper.

'Your shot, Billy,' his opponent shouts above the din. 'If you can leave it alone.'

'Okay, I know.' He picks up his cue again.

'You're snookered.' His friend is grinning at his own cleverness.

'We'll see about that.' Billy takes a couple of minutes to move around the table lining up his shot. The ball hits the cushion at a good angle and though it doesn't slide into the pocket he taps it sufficiently to put himself in a playing position. He walks towards Martha while his companion plays his shot. 'Have another drink,' he says to her, his eyes moving slowly around her face. 'I'll finish this game quickly and then we'll go and talk somewhere.' He pushes his way to the bar to refill her glass and his own.

He retrieves the coins on the pool-table edge. 'I won't have another game if you don't mind, mate,' he says when they've finished the game. 'Another time. Maybe tomorrow? Yes? Good.' He takes Martha's hand and guides her through the crowd and outside – slightly drunk, and gulping in the fresh, cold fifth-of-November air. 'Rockets,' says Billy. 'Let's send up a rocket,' he whispers, right up close into her ear. 'Just one. I know somewhere quiet not far from here.'

'We don't have any,' she laughs.

'I got a rocket in my pocket.' He pulls it out. 'Look.' They walk, hand in hand, towards the park. 'And I've got something else for you.'

The rocket goes up perfectly straight, bright and with a rush of sound that enhances their already excited state.

'Let's go an' have another drink,' says Martha.

'No.' He is confident. 'No, I know what I'm doing.'

The emergence of a realization in Billy that sobering-up

would better serve both of them meant that they had to have something to eat. Though this caution is not characteristic of him, even he, occasionally, is capable of doing the right thing. Besides, someone has told Billy, it is much more fun if you are not too drunk. And prolonging the moment before he has his way excites him. 'We'll get some chips,' he says.

Martha's legs find their normal equilibrium after their snack. But the alcohol remaining in the bloodstream has the effect of taking the unpleasant edge off reality and replacing it with a softer world altogether – a place where sensuality might be unrestrained, where they might come together.

The only obstacle is a practical one on a damp night. Billy's hostel is out of the question. That leaves Martha's room, 'guarded,' Martha says, 'by an old she-dog landlady, with eyes as big as saucers.' It isn't that Mrs Wall is against hedonistic satisfactions of the flesh, nor is she even shy about her own exploits. There is always at least one of her lodgers who enjoys privileges denied the others. And it isn't jealousy of Martha's youth and attractiveness, for Mrs Wall is oblivious to aesthetic qualities in others. She has a curious puritan notion, a set of morals whose code is known only to herself. Her censoriousness will suddenly leap on a foible of human behaviour and, with no obvious logic, condemn it.

'No way,' says Martha, 'would she allow you to stay the night.'

It is late, as they stand listening. Mrs Wall has a problem which frequently disturbs her lodgers, but, as Martha tells Billy, can be turned to their advantage. She snores. It isn't just a quiet hiss of breath through blocked or resisting tubes, or a soft grating of air passing congested old pipes, or vibration rattling the palate of dentures. It is a rhythmic sound which resembles most the noise emitted from a blocked drain as the water is released by a plunger – as if she is sucking in bits of the world, under pressure, at regular intervals.

They tip-toe, softly giggling, ears alerted, towards Martha's room. The slurp of Mrs Wall's snores reassures them of her ignorance of their rule-breaking. Tomorrow Billy's exit will present another problem. Neither of them is prepared, in any sense of the word, for the pleasure that awaits them.

He brushes his teeth with her toothbrush, standing at the mean basin in her room. He turns and she notices a smear of toothpaste at the corner of his mouth. She reaches up, and slowly and tenderly wipes it away with her finger. It is a concentrated, clear gannet-cry of sensuality. He leans forward and delicately touches her mouth with his death-cold damp lips. She breathes life into him; warms his mouth with hers. The passion of it takes them both aback.

'You want to make love?' he says, so quietly she thinks she imagines it. Was he really asking? Not leaping or pouncing on her like she thinks Lisa's friends do on her.

'No,' she says, 'I'm frightened.'

'It'll be all right.' His arms cradle her waist. She puts hers around his neck and he lifts her inches off the ground and walks to the bed.

He takes off his shirt. She notices the long vein down the side of his neck, pumping. The muscles on his arms tighten as he unzips his trousers and lets them fall. He steps out of them. His flat, firm belly leads down to his erect penis, with a drop on the tip glistening a welcome.

'Now you,' he says, his eyes gleaming and a smile so full of affection she feels a treacherous security.

Her nipples taste pale pink and slightly salted. He nestles between her breasts and then noses up again on to her mouth. Her tongue replies to his darting, with a soft encouragement. He is on top of her. Her legs part, falling relaxed and then flexing as she pushes her thighs together against his, feeling the downy skin of his legs as he rubs against her belly.

'I've never done it before,' he says.

'Me neither. So be careful. You got to be careful the first time, you know.'

'I know,' he says. He lifts himself on to his elbow, leaning to one side. 'It'll be all right then. You'll see.' His hand is slowly stroking her pubic hair, and then he delicately parts the lips.

'I have to get you wet down there, before I come in.' His fingers stroke her, caressing her so delicately they almost hover above the moistening lips. Only intuition could have spawned such a sensitive lover, and the power of feeling is making them both responsive to every nuance. She is ready for him.

Her movements correspond to his thrusts, and in the next room Mrs Wall's reassuring snores keep time. They hear the sound of the windrush, the roar of excitement as he takes off, flapping, flapping, soaring high. And she, very nearly. But at least she flutters, and almost flies.

13

'GOOD-NIGHT, THEN.' Lisa holds the door open as he waves from the top of the stairs. 'Thanks for the drink.'

'See you around. I'll see myself out of the front door,' Frank says unnecessarily. She had no intention of leaving the warmth of her room. ''bye.'

She readies herself for bed. She is disappointed he hasn't spent the night with her. She knew from the way he looked at her and by the turns and twists of conversation it was in his mind. She fancied him, and was in the mood for a good screw. She would have been more direct with him and suggested he stay, but she recognized he was the sort of bloke who needs to make the first move or he wouldn't think he was having fun. She slips naked under the covers, turns on the bedside lamp, and lights a cigarette. There is a creaking noise from a loose floorboard outside the door followed by a tentative tapping. 'Yes,' she says in a hoarse whisper.

'Can I come in?' He peers around the edge of the door.
'Yes.'

He shuts the door, walks to the bed, hesitates a minute,

and lies down fully clothed beside her. He leaves one shoe against the other before kicking them both off.

'Well?' she says.

'You don't mind me coming back?'

'Does it look like it?'

'No.'

'Why are you lying beside me with your clothes on?'

'I don't know.'

'Yes, you do.'

'Yes, I suppose I do.'

'Take them off then.'

Very tasty too, thinks Lisa, slipping out from the rumpled and disorganized mound of covers in the morning. She turns to see if she has wakened him, and notices a frown on his sleeping face. Sleeping beauty, she smiles to herself, remembering how she used to believe all the old myths. She slips on a robe and slippers and, walking to the bathroom, considers the lie. The prince kisses the sleeping beauty and she wakes up. No she doesn't, thinks Lisa, she bloody falls asleep. She wanders around in a moony daze, oblivious to the faults of the wandering prince, suppressing her own ambitions and slugged out cold in a soporific state. Women aren't the only ones who behave this way, she admits to herself. Her old friend Charlie is like a pet dog, always wagging his tail at her and sitting up and begging, though she has no time for him. She just throws him the odd bone and he barks in response. Dogs are always repeating themselves. She smiles and fills the basin with water.

A bath would be nice but there isn't time so she'll just wash all over. She loves the smell of herself after sex, pity to get rid of it. She removes her dutch cap before washing and patting it dry and placing it in its white container. She likes her dome-shaped rubber protector because she's in charge of it and it doesn't fill her body with either drugs or unwanted brats. She finishes washing and makes two cups of coffee in the small kitchenette. She takes one to Frank.

'Mmmm,' he says, 'why don't you get back into bed?'

'I'll be late for work.'

'What's the time?'

'Eight.'

'Christ!' He sits upright suddenly, shaking his head. 'I'd better get organized, too.' He takes the cup. 'Thanks.' He sips the coffee.

'You can use the bathroom now.' She nods towards the door. 'I've used it already and there's no one else in there yet.' She begins to dress. 'Better hurry before someone else in the house gets up.'

He is out of bed, his arms around her half-naked body, drawing her closer, nuzzling her hair with his face. He is making moaning noises. 'Mmmmm, mmmm,' he goes.

'You'd better hurry,' she says. 'There's a bloke downstairs takes ages when he gets into the bathroom.' She pushes him away. 'You don't want to be late for work, eh?'

'Doesn't this mean anything to you?' He moves back towards her.

'Mean anything? What are you on about?' She pulls on her slip. 'How can it mean anything? I hardly know you, we were both drunk, but it was very nice and thank you.'

'God, you're hard.' He picks up his trousers, bends down, and searches around for his shoes, which have somehow walked under the bed. He straightens up, holding his shoes and bunched, crumpled clothes together. 'You'd go with anyone, wouldn't you?'

'I resent that. No, I wouldn't. I wouldn't go with anyone I didn't fancy. You don't know me at all. I'll tell you what it means to me. I find you attractive, you turn me on. I don't

102

see how you can find that offensive, and I resent your bloody attitude. I only know you on a surface level, so it's only a surface response, okay? You are a nice bit of crumpet.'

A nice bit of crumpet! 'Streuth, he muses as he dashes for the bathroom, and grins at the thought of what the school governors would say if they could hear this description of him. How will it look on his C.V. when he applies for the post of Deputy Head, next week? Frank Hawkins, teacher in a comprehensive school, B.Sc., M.Sc., H.Dip Ed., N.B.O.C. (Nice Bit of Crumpet).

Friday is always the most frantic day at the café, with customers being parted from their well-earned cash, tired and impatient on payday. It never occurs to the manager, Dick, to offer additional help when the place is packed; rather he sits on a stool at the corner of the counter, by the till, getting in the way and gratuitously pointing out waiting customers to Lisa and Martha. Someone is using the one-armed bandit and an irritating clatter comes through. It is difficult keeping the oilcloths on the table well wiped when the demand for service is at its height. Dick points out someone waiting for service on table four.

'Do it yourself, you wanker,' Martha snaps, pouring coffee for another customer waiting at the counter.

'Martha, please, just get on with it.' He straightens himself on the stool. 'No cheek,' he leers, and gives her bottom a slap as she passes with the coffee. 'Like a good girl.'

'Take this.' She hands the coffee to the person waiting for it. 'It's on the house.' She turns towards Dick. 'You,' she says, hands on hips, 'are disgusting. You stink like the rubbish we chuck out,' she screams, silencing the room.

'You're fired,' he says, standing up from the stool.

'Good.' She walks to the till and presses the key to open it, removes two big notes, and slams it shut. 'My wages. Thanks.' She rushes through to the kitchen, which faces onto a side lane, busy with people passing the open window. They turn to watch as he shouts, 'Come back here.' He grabs her arm. 'You can't just walk out, and you can't help yourself to money like that.'

'Watch me.' She stuffs the money down her bra.

'Calm down.' He follows her to the kitchen door. 'If you want a break from the front, wash some of the dishes.' He grabs her wrist. 'Do you hear me?'

'I hear you,' she says. 'Something about taking a break, washing dishes. Let me have my arm back.' She bites the arm which is holding hers, gives him a smack on the face with the released hand, and picks up a plate waiting to be washed, crashes it down on his head, and sees him slide to the floor, accompanied by the shattered plate. She turns towards the window, where people are enjoying the performance. For Act Two, she opens the window and, taking one plate at a time, hurls them out until the entire pile disappears. She laughs as people duck to avoid them. Dick is groaning.

'Washing up is finished.' She steps over the limp figure, wipes her hands in the air, and leaves to find Billy.

'I've left me job,' she says. 'I don't know what I'm going to do for rent.' She tells him of her parting gestures.

'Great!' He laughs. 'I think you and I might have the angels on our side.'

'What do you mean?'

'Well, as luck has it, one of me mates got drunk, stole a car, and then tried to park it in the back seat of a stationary police wagon waiting at a red traffic light. When so rudely interrupted, he fell out of the driver's seat into the welcoming arms of the Old Bill. It isn't the first time he's been in trouble and he got sent down for eighteen months.' He is rolling a joint.

'I don't get you. What's in it for us?'

Billy takes a key out of his pocket and holds it in front of Martha's face. 'We can use his room until he gets out.' He waves the key and then puts it back in his pocket. 'He said so.'

'How long?' Martha looks anxious.

'A year minimum. Eighteen months if he doesn't behave himself and loses his remission.' He licks the cigarette paper and smooths it.

'Sounds okay to me.' She looks down. 'Mrs Wall will discover you eventually, anyway, Billy. Bound to.' She looks away from him. Mrs Wall has so far remained unaware of the romance unfolding each night in Martha's room, and ignorant of the ingenuity with which Billy engineers his escape each morning via a trusty drainpipe. 'There's something else too.'

'What?'

'I think I'm pregnant.'

'What?'

'You heard.'

'Christ, how could you do this to me?'

'What do you mean, do it to you?' She looks at him, tears welling up.

'I'm sorry, girl.' He touches her arm nervously. 'I didn't mean it.'

'You'll have to get a regular job, now, won't you? If you are going to be someone's father it wouldn't be right to go on dealing. I don't think I could stand all your junkie friends around our baby.'

Fortunately the rent is low on their gangster friend's room.

105

Billy finds a job on the site with Charlie, there is a meter for electricity, and Billy supplements their income, amid Martha's protestations, with shop-lifting. As her pregnancy progresses she prepares for the baby, collecting small clothes which she puts away carefully in a chest she has bought second-hand at the market. But she wants a pram for it, and there isn't enough money for such an item.

'It's not so easy,' says Billy, sitting down and untying his shoes after a hard day's work. 'I've had a look and they're all linked by a chain in the local shop.'

'You can't nick one, Billy.'

'That's what I'm saying. Mind you, I think I've worked out a satisfactory answer.' He begins to wash off the day's grime. 'I've been sussing out Sainsbury's.' He splashes cold water onto his face. 'We'll get the usual shopping tonight and then have a look around the back where they park the kids in their prams.' He turns to look at her, towel in hand. 'You choose whichever one you like and we'll turf the contents out and leave the kid in a trolley.' He laughs. 'Clever, eh? That way we'd have blankets and a mattress for it too.' He throws down a towel. 'It's a fine night so the kid won't catch cold.'

'That's not funny, Billy. Who knows what might happen to the kid?'

'C'mon, don't be so serious. I think it's a very constructive idea. They'll find the brat when they leave.'

'Piss-off.' She grabs her coat. 'It's an evil idea.'

'You want a pram, don't you?'

'Help,' she says, letting out a wail. 'I'm just going for a walk. I can't stand being in the same room as someone so callous.' She moans to herself as she slips down the steps, turning her back on him and facing the desolate memories of her own beginnings.

When it is quite dark she returns and slips into bed beside his sleeping body. She hasn't anywhere else to go, has she?

106

14

IT IS A normal birth: the pain so intense she feels as if she is being filleted alive. They give her a drug to ease it; she feels the same sensations but cannot protest. Finally, through the pain and bright lights, during an entrance which takes Martha's breath away, Sally looks in on the world; slithering, blinking, wet, warm, and noisy. Cradling her tiny daughter in her arms, Martha quite simply falls in love with her. When he holds her later, Billy looks as if he's been knocked by a truck.

Frank has kept in touch throughout the pregnancy and sends flowers to the hospital. He visits her the day following her release.

'Any time you need any help or advice let me know.' He smiles. 'You only have to ask.' He waves his hands in the air. 'Don't leave it till you're desperate.' He purses his lips and makes a cooing noise. 'Very sweet child.'

For years Frank has had the uneasy feeling that despite his obvious attractions – status, secure job, charming manner – he might remain on the shelf. Stacked there labelled 'free'. Available and willing but somehow unclaimed. One of the deviants of society. He is very fond of small children, displaying a tolerance and warmth not shown by every man. It would be hard to find anyone more suitable as a father. He contemplates the irony of the unsuitable Billy (and, indeed, reluctant and ungrateful Billy) enjoying the fruits of his lustful loins without appreciating his good fortune. He must try to help them. There is much he can teach them, much he can teach their child. Good, kind Uncle Frank.

Lisa visits Martha frequently when she first leaves hospital. But the visits dwindle as she gets bored with baby talk, and frightened by seeing her friend trapped all day and night in a world so apparently limited in interest. Charlie comes to see them on his own and offers to babysit, until Billy becomes suspicious of his solicitousness towards his family and sees him off. He takes Charlie for a walk and tells him that Martha is fed up with him dropping by. The smile leaves Charlie's face.

Billy thinks: he's a sly bugger. Lisa's right, you can't trust his good nature; it's a disguise for something else. He's not as stupid as he makes out. Martha thinks differently. Charlie isn't deliberately obtuse from some cunning or calculating reason. He's truly thick. But he's sensitive and kind. She misses watching the gentle way he handles the baby.

Time is running out on the flat. Billy's mate is due out of prison soon. At first Billy rejects Charlie's offer to share his room, but as it becomes evident that they haven't found anywhere and his mate's release from the nick is imminent, Billy accepts. Three adults and a baby in one room.

When he isn't working Billy spends much of his time drinking, playing snooker, or making obscene telephone calls. When he returns late in the evenings he works out on his chest expander and other exercises for half an hour. He still daydreams of flying, of excitement and danger. Martha, frustrated by her isolation, doesn't disguise her contempt for this activity. Charlie often goes to the pub to watch in dismay as Lisa enjoys herself with other lads. 'I'll have my own place back when the others have found somewhere,' he tells her. 'Then you can come and stay with me again.'

'I don't understand why you let them push you around,' she says. 'They're taking advantage of you. What about me, eh?' She looks angry. 'Or is there something else going on?'

'What do you mean?' he says.

Martha knows she will have to start the search for somewhere better to live. Locked in the cramped conditions, her relationship with Billy deteriorates. She is exhausted by the baby's demands but her maternal feelings are strong enough to repress her desire to flee the situation.

She is desperate now. She goes to the school at the end of the afternoon, catching Frank's attention when he leaves. The Hawk happily takes her under his wing, driving her to the Housing Department of the local City Council offices. He stays with her while they deal with her case, encouraging her, helping to fill in the forms. Eventually, Martha, Billy, and Sally are moved into a room for homeless families. Even Billy admits Frank has been useful. But gratitude is an uneasy bedfellow for suspicion; Billy has no smooth veneer to conceal hostility. 'There's a catch in it somewhere,' he says.

Frank helps Martha find a second-hand cot. He paints each rung a different colour. 'Babies need stimulation,' he says, washing the brushes in turps. 'Never forget that, Martha.' As well as food and space, she thinks darkly. He sits watching her move around the room, first making two mugs of tea, then folding the baby's things, putting them on top of the tiny chest of drawers. Sally lies on the bed.

'Better leave the window open by the cot.' He pulls it up a few inches, finds a jam-jar, and wedges it open. 'The paint fumes won't be good for any of you.' He turns around.

'It'll get cold in here.' Martha puts a blanket over the child.

'Well, you haven't much choice until the paint is dry.' He rubs his hands together. 'It'll only be for a few hours.' He looks around the room. 'Take her for a walk in the pram, it's a nice day.'

'I haven't got a pram.' She pulls her cardigan across her chest and folds her arms.

'No, of course not.' He is buttoning his coat. 'I'd better get going.' He walks to the bed and pats the baby. 'She's lovely, you must be proud of her.' His hand is on the door. 'Take care of yourself.' He opens the door.

'Hello,' says Billy, standing, legs apart, in the open doorway, swaying slightly.

'I'm just off,' says Frank, passing Billy, and directing one arm towards the room. 'Martha has a surprise for you.' And he's off, taking the stairs two at a time.

'Very nice.' Billy is sweating. He slams the door behind him as he enters the room.

'What's he talking about, eh?' His eyes shift towards the cot, and turn back to Martha sitting on the bed, stroking the baby's feet.

'He helped me find the cot.' She nods towards it. 'It's second-hand, only a few quid. He painted it for me.' She's looking at Sally. 'She's moving around now and needs a cot.' She gets up.

'Why is he so interested?'

'Why shouldn't he be? Look, Billy, we don't have too many friends. At least he got this place for us and bought the cot for Sally. There isn't anyone else who's as decent to us.' She turns her back towards him while she smooths the bed with her hands.

'You could ask yourself why he's doing it. What's it to him? Do you think he cares about us? What's in it for him, I said?'

'You're so suspicious. He knows the right people to help us and he can afford to buy things because he doesn't have any family and has a decent job.'

'So he paid for the cot, did he?'

'Yes.'

'He's not doing it for me. He's doing it for you.'

'Oh shut up!' She fills the kettle noisily. 'He's kind, generous. That's all.'

'Nobody does anything for anyone for nothing.' He is scratching at a spot on his chin.

'You're wrong again. He may be a bit odd but he really likes doin' things for people. He told me so.' She fetches the baby's bottle and scoops powdered milk into it. Sally is whimpering on the bed.

'Oh, he's a worthy one he is. Cornered the market in worthiness. All-purpose worthy person. Says he likes doin' things for people. Pretentious fucker.' A flash of red blood oozes from the spot.

'I asked him to help!' She swings around, faces him, and slams the bottle down on to the table. 'You could say I took advantage of him. No bloody body ever cared for you or me unless they were paid to do so, right? Well, if you want anything in this world, Billy Watts, you've got to be cunning and find out – well, find out . . .' – she puts the bottle in a cracked jug and pours cold water around the edge – 'I don't know, find out who's likely to do you a good turn when you need it.'

'You're an opportunist.' There are no questions on his face. 'Now I see. Don't be surprised if he wants something

111

from you.' He forgets to close his mouth; it is slack and slightly open and only closes when she says, 'Here, feed the baby,' and hands him the bottle.

'This,' says Martha, holding up a mixture of tea leaves and hair, 'is the fag-end of life.' She works at the plug-hole again, freeing it of its slimy contents until the water goes down. 'It smells bloody awful.' She washes her hands, trying to scrub away the memory of the debris. She feels too grubby to eat the bread and tea which is their meal. They have been in the room for three months now and the initial enthusiasm is wearing thin. She avoids glancing at the bucket, filled with water and stinking nappies, lurking in the corner of the room; she must wash them before going to bed or there will be none for the baby tomorrow. She hangs them around the table edge to dry. If she leaves them in the bathroom they share with the other families, as likely as not one goes missing. She's fed-up about the number of rows it has caused. At least in the Home there had always been enough to eat and wear and no shortage of sheets or blankets. She wishes she knew how to sew so she could make some clothes for Sally.

'Charlie and me will be made redundant unless we go to Birmingham.' Crumbs fall from Billy's mouth as he eats. 'The building company's got a contract up there.' He looks at Martha, who is strolling up and down the small room with Sally over her shoulder. The baby blinks in surprise every time she passes the naked light-bulb. Martha stops under the light and Sally squirms and frets.

'We can't go up there. We're only just settled here. When does the job finish?'

'Two weeks' time. Charlie says he might follow them to Birmingham. There's no work around here. He's free to go, lucky bugger.'

'You haven't looked for another job. You'll find something if you make an effort.' She shakes her head. 'Poor Charlie. He won't like moving. He'd like to be in your shoes. He'd like to have a family to work for, like you. Someone to call his own.' She hands the child to Billy.

'How would you know?' he says, putting the baby over his shoulder and jerking it up and down. 'You been seeing him or something?'

'No, of course not. I know Charlie. Lisa talks about him sometimes. He'd do anything to settle down with her.'

'Well, why doesn't he then, if he's so keen?'

'She's not interested.'

'He hasn't got enough money for her fancy tastes.' The baby is crying.

'Well, if she says so. I never heard her say that.'

'She doesn't have to, idiot. It's obvious.'

'Well, at least she's honest. Even if she hasn't said it, and just thinks it, at least she's honest about what she thinks. Sensible too, probably.' She leans towards him. 'Give her here.' She takes the child. 'At least she has a good time, which is more than can be said for some.' She sighs.

'You got yourself into this bloody mess. Me too.' He stands up and leans over her.

'Go away.' She gently pushes him with her forearm.

'I said, you got us in this mess.' He bends forward and shouts in her ear. 'I didn't want it. I didn't want it. I didn't want it.' He backs away.

'That's very smart, Billy. How long are you going to keep up this rubbish? I'm tired of hearing the same old complaint. It doesn't help. It doesn't solve anything to go on and on and on. Grow up!' she says, looking at the child.

'You can't get away with that.' He is agitated, rocking backwards and forwards on his feet. 'You've trapped me.' He bends forwards again. 'You've bloody trapped me. You got pregnant deliberately. You wanted the baby, and I'm a sucker. Just a bloody, fucking sucker. I wanted to be free, to travel and see things. There's countries all over the world. Places, incredible places, places you can't even imagine they're so different. So different from this bloody hole' – he surveys the room – 'with screaming kids, neighbours that are half bonkers, blinkin' savages, stinkin' nappies, blocked bloody drains, the meter always runnin' out, an' cockroaches scamperin' and tappin' all night long as if they was trying to dig their way out. I don't blame them if they are. Who'd want to stay in this dump?'

'I'm hungry,' she says, sadly recognizing the truth of what he is saying.

'I'll go and get some fish and chips.' He fingers the change in his pocket. 'I got to make a couple of phone calls first. You know, see if I can find another job. I'll get the evening paper and have a look. You never know.' He goes towards the door. 'I might get lucky.'

'Hello.'

'Hello.'

'Mrs Watts?'

'Yes, who's that?'

'It's your son here, Mrs Watts.'

'I doubt it. He's just crawled behind the sofa a minute ago and he can't talk yet. You must have the wrong number.'

'Yeah. I suppose so.' Billy replaces the receiver and kicks the door open. Another wasted call. He hasn't had a decent chat for weeks.

15

HE SCRUTINIZES HIS face in the mirror and taps it dry with a
warm towel. Not bad. He has just opened this morning's
post, which has the written confirmation of his appointment as Deputy Head of the school. He lifts the slackening
muscles with a grin. Better. Well, it's more responsibility,
but there's no turning back: it's what he wanted. Now for a
bit of after-shave and he's ready. Who can he take along
with him tonight to wine and dine and celebrate? Damn.
Frank nearly catches his fingers in the door as he
remembers he's arranged to meet Billy this evening. Why
did he make these arrangements when he should have
known that it would be an evening of celebration, that
today the good news of his appointment would be con-
firmed in writing? Some strange fascination drew him to
Billy, and he didn't understand it. Was it that Billy
awakened a dormant but incipient paternal feeling? Or was
it the natural extension of his commitment as a teacher?

He contemplates the possibility of encouraging Billy into
further education, but is worried about how to approach
him, because he recalls his resolute resistance to learning.

He will remember to treat Billy as an equal, not patronize him; see the best in him, not deny him his responsibilities. It is a question, he thinks, of waiting for the small signals that indicate when he might usefully guide him without being offensive, steer him towards making decisions without intruding with his own opinions too overtly. Someone else's inadequacy determined a bad hand of cards for Billy.

Frank remembers his own childhood and how he followed his parents' advice through school, college, and sensible career. It mattered to him that they approved. He had fulfilled their predictions and ambitions for him, never stopping to question them. They trimmed his behaviour with continuous nudges of criticism. They'll be pleased when he tells them of his new success, his new appointment at the school. And one day, when he becomes Head Teacher, well, they'll be really proud of him then.

'You look well tonight,' Frank takes off his jacket and places it around the back of a chair. 'What do you want to drink?'

'A pint of bitter will do fine.' Billy crosses his legs, sitting in the chair opposite the jacket.

'What do you say to having one drink here and then going to have something to eat?' He places a pint carefully on a beer-mat in front of Billy.

'It would be fine with me if I had any money.' Billy turns the glass around on the mat. 'I've been made redundant unless I move to Birmingham. Martha doesn't want to go. But there's nothing else here.'

'Yes, I see. Don't worry about paying for the meal, that's my treat. I've had a bit of luck. But the other thing's a problem. I'm sure you're worried.'

'The dole money doesn't go very far. She'll soon get fed up always being broke.' He gulps down half his beer. They are both silent.

'If you move you'll lose your place on the housing waiting-list.' Frank breaks the silence. 'Well, perhaps that's not strictly accurate. I don't think Martha would lose the place here if she stayed.' He leans forward, elbows on the arms of the chair, hands clasped together. 'If you had a choice, what would you really like to do?'

'Never thought about it. Anything that made a bit of money.' Billy finishes his drink.

'Anything legal, you mean,' says Frank, eyebrows raised expectantly.

'Legal or illegal, I don't mind.' Billy laughs. 'Why are you so bloody interested, anyway?'

'I don't know.' Frank leans back and folds his arms.

'Martha is talking about getting a job.'

'What will you do about the baby?' Frank asks.

'I don't know. She'll have to sort that out.' Billy is folding the beer-mat. 'Perhaps Hilda will look after her. She's already got her own child to mind anyway. You remember, the woman that lived above Martha at Mrs Wall's? No, perhaps you wouldn't know her. Enough of that, let's go and eat, I'm hungry.'

'Anything you fancy you can have. Don't worry about the expense. I'm paying, remember.' Frank laughs as he hands the menu to Billy.

'Ta.' Billy studies it. He has been here before with some of his contacts during the time he was a dealer. The waiter nods his recognition of Billy, to Frank's surprise.

'Smart car you have,' Billy says. The waiter stands behind Frank's chair, raising his eyebrows as a signal that he has something to discuss with Billy. Billy nods towards the door to the kitchen. Frank catches the response and turns around.

'Everything all right?' the waiter asks him.

'Fine, fine, thank you.' He turns back to Billy. 'What's going on?'

117

'Nothing,' he grins. 'Bloody great place.'

'Yes, it is.' Frank is rubbing his nose. 'Tell me, what will you find to do all day, every day?'

'Plenty.'

'Very remarkable. But not very specific, eh? What I mean is, I'd find it very difficult to fill my time if I didn't teach, and of course the money is useful too.' He hesitates, a forkful of food close to his mouth. 'But perhaps that's a disadvantage from my point of view. Always having a structured day and not being resourceful, in a sense. People like me would be helpless if we were out of work because we are so used to the routine. We'd be thrown off balance without it. Do you see?' He pushes the food into his mouth.

'Sounds as if you have a problem there.' Billy takes a sip of wine. 'Of course if someone offered me something I liked doing for a decent wage I'd consider it. But I can't see that happening.' He raises his voice. 'I get knackered on the building site and what for? I work my balls off.' He is almost shouting, grinning as Frank winces and other diners pretend not to hear. 'After they've taxed and insured you, there's fuck-all left. Certainly not enough to put a bleedin' deposit down on one of the houses I've been building.' He gulps down the rest of the wine.

'You didn't ever consider getting some sort of training then? The exam results were no indication of your intelligence. I never knew anyone waste so much time at school as you did. We all know you're very bright, Billy.'

'We, who's we?' Billy turns around in all directions in a fake search.

'Anyone who taught you said the same thing.' Frank wipes his mouth with a napkin.

'Leave it out, will you,' says Billy, leaning forward. 'Forget about school.' He sits upright again and pushes his finger tips against the table. 'What about yourself then?

118

You contented with yourself, Frank?' He leans towards Frank again, fists clenched. 'Listen, mate, I resent you questioning the way I arrange my life. Martha may welcome your interference but I do not.'

'I didn't mean any offence. But it seems to me you've boxed yourself in to an almost intractable situation and, as an old friend, and with my experience, I wondered if there was anything I could do.' He leans back, arms behind his head.

'Well, you can always lend us a few quid.' Billy is mopping up the plate with a piece of bread. 'Delicious,' he says.

'That is not what I had in mind.'

'Well, it's what I have in mind.'

'Okay, okay. Yes, of course, if that will help.' Frank picks at his teeth with a finger-nail. 'But it isn't a solution to the problem, is it? Only a short-term relief.'

'That'll do fine. I don't arrange my life before I've even begun to live it. I don't understand this preoccupation with the future. I could be dead tomorrow.'

'You are living on that assumption?'

'No, of course not. You are jumping to conclusions again. There is something in between the two extremes. You have your life so carefully planned out, I daresay you've even picked the colour from a chart for your wheelchair, the location of your retirement home, and the type of wood for your coffin.'

'You have a point, I'll concede.' Frank pours more wine into Billy's glass. 'I have a habit of seeking prescriptive solutions.'

'Oh yeah.' Billy wonders what Frank means. He is beginning to feel the effect of the wine. 'As far as I'm concerned I don't have any problems.' He notices the waiter staring at him. 'As I asked before, what about

119

yourself? Eh?' He stares into Frank's face and crosses his legs. 'I said, what about yourself?'

'Ah well, now that's a question. Where are you going?' he asks as Billy gets up.

'Just to the gents.'

'Oh.'

Billy heaves up into the bowl. He wipes a dribble of puke from his chin and rinses his mouth under the tap. He is just sober enough to take a paper towel and clean around the bowl before flushing it. He does this in order not to be discovered making a show of himself in case Frank might follow him, rather than with any consideration for anyone who might use the convenience later. The door opens and the waiter enters.

'No chance.' Billy puts his hands in his pockets and shakes his head. 'Too risky,' he says to the waiter. 'The price has gone sky high and I haven't got anything at the moment. If you want a supply you'll have to try someone else. Sorry I can't help you.' And he clutches the waiter's arm for a minute, pats it twice, grins, and returns to the restaurant.

'Better be getting along.' Frank looks at his watch. 'We must have another meal together soon.' He folds the bill over the cheque.

'Yes. Thanks a lot. I enjoyed myself,' says Billy. 'We can meet up for a drink during the week if you like.'

'Fine. I know where to find you anyway.' Frank puts on his jacket. 'Give my love to Martha.'

'Eh?'

'Give my best to Martha.'

'Okay.'

Two weeks later Martha finds employment at a warehouse packing catalogues for despatch to travel agencies in different areas of the country. She works with twenty women. The warehouse is like an aircraft hanger. It is made of corrugated steel, with skylights set in the roof on one side, and it is open at one end. Cases of unsorted catalogues are piled along the side without windows and there is a machine opposite which is used to bind the packages into batches and to cover them in plastic. There is another machine for sealing the ends of the plastic casing. In an adjacent office building, women work typing out the labels. The floor above the typists is carpeted and it is here that the managers hang out. In the warehouse there is a machine which dispenses tea and coffee for a charge. Next to it is a rack containing time-cards and a clock for clocking-in. The women in her section wear overalls. She is shy about talking to them at first. During the half-hour lunch-break one of the women sits beside her and offers her a cigarette.

'My arms ache something rotten,' says Martha.

'You'll get used to it. You won't notice it after a couple of weeks,' says Mary, puffing at her cigarette. 'By that time it'll be so bleedin' cold in here you won't feel your bleedin' arms anyway.' She laughs.

'Well, it's not exactly warm today, is it?'

'It'll get worse,' says Mary. 'And, by the way' – she nods towards the time-clock – 'you don't mind me telling you, do you? But as you're new, you know . . . make sure you're not more than two minutes late in the mornings or they'll deduct fifteen minutes' pay. You don't mind my telling you, do you?'

'No, oh no. Thanks. They didn't tell me that when I came in this morning.'

'They don't. They take it off anyway. They can make their own rules. No unions, you see. It's a small company, and when a couple of the lasses joined a union they sacked 'em. No problem replacing them, of course, because there's not much work around here.'

'Suppose I was three minutes late each day, it would be fifteen minutes total for the week, right?'

'They'd take off fifteen minutes' for each day. You'd lose one-and-a-quarter-hours' wages.'

'That's not fair.'

'No, it isn't, but that's the way they operate. Come on, we'd best get started again. There goes the siren.'

She collects Sally from Hilda on the way home.

'Mrs Wall's none too happy with our arrangement,' says Hilda. 'We should have asked her first, she said.'

'It's your room, you should be able to do what you like with it,' Martha says, Sally clinging to her neck, pecking her on the cheek with soft, wet kisses, her little hands moving gently across Martha's features, caressing them.

'Well, she hasn't said anything much. I think you better talk to her yourself.'

'We can't let this arrangement continue for too long, Martha,' Mrs Wall says when she goes to see her. 'After all, it is a disruption.'

'Could you give it a few weeks to see how things work out until I've had an opportunity to make other arrangements, do you think?' Martha is sitting in Mrs Wall's kitchen.

'Just for the moment then.' She takes Sally's hand in hers. 'She's a fine child.' Sally grins in response.

'She seems to like you.'

Martha gets up at 6.30 every morning. She changes and feeds Sally, packs her nappies and bottles, slips her own sandwiches into a plastic bag, and with baby in one arm and bags in the other, gets to Hilda by 7.15. That leaves her forty-five minutes to get to work at 8 am. If the bus is late she will lose money. She leaves work at 5 pm, arriving

122

home, after collecting Sally, at 7 pm. As she discovers, it is too late to do any shopping. Hilda offers to do this for her sometimes. So before she goes to work Martha must make out a shopping-list to slip in with the baby's things. After working for a month she invests some of her wages in a second-hand pushchair and this makes it much easier to manage, because Sally is getting heavy to carry.

Martha notices that Hilda is silent and troubled-looking sometimes. Her hair needs a wash and she doesn't look at Martha as she hands Sally to her. Martha is torn between sympathy for Hilda and her own need to have Hilda mind Sally. So she doesn't ask Hilda what is the matter. The situation for Billy has become difficult. He spends mornings in the Job Centre searching unsuccessfully for work and his afternoons drinking and making furtive telephone calls. All part of the life of a small-time dealer.

16

'YOU ARE LOOKING tired, Hilda,' Mrs Wall says. 'Too much for you, is it, coping with two children?'

'I know you don't like the arrangement.' Patronizing bitch, thinks Hilda pushing her hair away from her face. 'But I need the money Martha gives me for minding Sally and she can't work if I don't look after her child.'

'Why doesn't Billy look after Sally?'

'I don't know.'

'Well, why don't you suggest it? It's his responsibility too, and he isn't working, is he?'

'No.'

'Well then?'

'What about me? I've become dependent on the few extra pounds a week, and besides I like Sally.'

'The arrangement really can't last. I told Martha when she started work. Perhaps there is a play group or nursery school around here which could take the child.'

'No nursery school would take her for the long hours Martha works even if one existed around here, which it doesn't. Anyway, Timmy likes the company of Sally, too, and it's good for both of them.'

'Well, the arrangement cannot continue. I can't tolerate
the extra noise and fuss. I have my other tenants to
consider, as you know. You must let Martha know that I'll
only let the arrangement stand for another week and no
more. That gives her time to make other arrangements for
herself.' Mrs Wall looks at Hilda. 'It's for your own good
too, of course. You really are looking very tired, and we
don't want you to get ill under the strain. You know that
you're not very strong. You have to care for yourself and
little Timmy first.'

'I'm walking out of here unless they provide some heating.
It's too fucking cold to work.' Martha rubs her numb hands.
There are chilblains on three of her fingers and one of them
has split and is oozing. She tries to breathe some warmth
into them, cupping her hands around her mouth and
blowing.

'No chance,' says Mary, 'we've tried before. Nothing
doing. They said, we must work harder and we'll keep
warm. As if we don't already. What can we say to that, eh?'

'I'll bloody tell them.' Martha pushes her hands into the
pockets of her anorak. The temperature outside has
dropped below freezing, and the wind has blown the snow
into the open side of the warehouse all morning. They have
to move the equipment a distance from the open side
because the snow will spoil the brochures.

'Let's go and talk to Rock Hudson, then.' Rock is the
nickname for the boss. His secretary is called Doris (Day) by
the women. This is because she flirts with him and goes for
little drinks at lunchtime. 'She thinks she's going to work
her way up through the management,' says Mary. 'You
know what she said when she first joined? She said, "I'm
moving up, mark my words," as if I cared!'

Rock and Doris are the subject of elaborate stories exchanged by the women in which they speculate on the amorous adventures and manipulative games of the pair, what working your way up through management involves, and what he does with his plonker in the lift between floors – bringing a new definition to upwardly mobile. They are very crude, and take it in turns to contribute daily episodes to the soap serial they have titled 'Rock on Doris'.

'What are we going to do about the cold?' Cathy says.

'I think we should all walk out,' says Sheila.

'Great suggestion, Sheila. That'll get us a long way,' Mary says sarcastically. 'Wait till he gets back from his wet lunch, have another word with him if he's a bit boozed up, and then if he pays no attention we can leave in front of him. It won't work at all if he isn't here to witness it. You know how sour he is anyway. But with a few drinks inside him he might be better-humoured.' She looks around at the others. 'Who's going to tell him?'

'Wait to see who he asks,' says Sheila. 'Any one of us can give it to him straight, right?'

They start work again after the lunch break. Rock arrives back at three o'clock. They are working in their coats because it is so cold, and they put their hands in their pockets as he arrives, and begin to move away from the work area towards the door.

'Where do you think you're going?' he says.

'Home.'

He looks at his watch, moving his wrist back and forth till he's sure he's focussing correctly. 'It's only three o'clock.'

'It's too cold to work,' says Cathy, who is standing close to him.

'You should smell his breath,' she whispers to Sheila, hand covering her mouth. She coughs to disguise the comment and gesture.

126

'Ladies,' he starts again, looking around at the faces before him. 'I've told you before, if you work hard you'll keep warm.'

'We tried that,' shouts Martha. 'It's still too cold, however fast we move, and most of the time we aren't walking about, just standing and moving our arms and hands.'

'Who are you?' He moves towards her. He is very little taller than Martha, so his head goes up in order that he can peer through half-closed eyes down at her. He folds his arms, standing legs apart.

'Martha.'

'Well, Martha. If you don't like it here you know what to do.'

'Yes,' she says, 'and I'm doing it. Leaving.' She turns away, and the other women follow her towards the door.

'Hold it,' he says, raising one hand, 'not all of you.' They keep walking. 'You, missy, stop,' he shouts. They all stop and turn around.

'If she goes, we all go,' says Sheila.

'Come here.' He is pointing at Martha; he crooks his finger and beckons. 'I've got an urgent order.' He looks her up and down. 'And it's got to go out today.' He looks at his watch again. 'Two hours, that's all the time we've got to complete it.'

'That's your problem,' says Martha. 'We can't work like this. Look at the snow blowin' in, and the cold goes right through us.' She holds out her hands. 'Look at those chilblains.'

'Very nasty, yes. Look, we're just one big family here.' The women grin at each other. 'That's the way I want to run the little business. Of course I have your best interests at heart, and we can't have you working in uncomfortable conditions.'

'It's impossible to work without heaters,' says Cathy.

127

'All right then, I'll tell you what I'll do. I'll have a word with my co-director, Gordon, and we'll work something out that'll satisfy you, but I can't produce a solution out of thin air.' He smiles. 'I promise we'll improve things and get something organized. But in the meantime, back to work like good girls. We have to get the order out or there'll be no money to pay you.' He is not smiling any more. 'You don't want to lose your money, do you? You have to remember I keep you all and but for me you wouldn't be taking home your nice fat wage packets, would you?'

'When are you going to do something?' says Martha.

'We'll have something worked out by tomorrow morning.' The boss is rubbing his hands and blowing on them. He begins to walk away.

'No,' says Mary. 'We'll give you one hour.' He turns back.

'Well, I don't know about all this urgency. But if you really feel so strongly, I'll be back in an hour, but get back to work in the meantime. I must say' – he raises his eyebrows – 'I think you're being very demanding.'

When he is out of earshot Cathy says, 'I don't trust him, he always procrastinates when it's a question of spending money on improvements.'

At four o'clock he arrives back with a cardboard carton and grins as he places it on the floor. 'There you are,' he says, 'as good as my word.' He begins to open it. 'Don't say I never do anything for you.' He takes out a balaclava helmet from the box and holds it up. He pulls it over Martha's resisting head.

'Is this the latest in industrial technology or something?' she says angrily. 'I must say I feel like a guerrilla.' She picks up a broom leaning against the wall and, tucking it under her arm, points it at him. 'Rat tat tat tat,' she says.

128

He backs away. 'Now, get us a heater or else.' He is not sure if she is joking or not.

'These won't solve the problem,' says Sheila, picking up one of the helmets. 'We need a heater.'

'There's no heater designed for a place this big,' he says, 'and besides' – he hands the women a helmet each – 'don't you know that eleven per cent of body heat is lost through a bare head? Well, it is, so you should be eleven per cent warmer wearing these.'

'We'll see,' says Sheila.

'Well, Sheila, luv, just give it to the end of the week. Give it a try at least.' He begins to leave. 'It'll be warmer soon, anyway, the weather forecast says so,' he shouts in parting.

'Bloody hell,' says Sheila. 'C'mon girls, let's get back to work.' Tears sparkle in her eyes. 'I'm going to enquire at the health and safety section down at the Job Centre. I'm sure he's lying, I'm sure he's breaking rules, and I'm sure they must have heaters for warehouses.' She turns to Cathy. 'Shit,' she says.

'Shit,' says Cathy, looking at the departing figure.

'If he sacks us there's plenty queuing up to take our places, right?' Sheila puts her arm around Cathy. 'Oh bugger, have a fag.' She hands her one. 'He won't show his nose around here till five, mean bugger.'

Martha never discovers whether the women did get a heater, or lost their jobs, or if things remained the same. When she arrives to collect Sally Hilda tells her what Mrs Wall has said about minding the baby for only one more week.

'I don't want to work there any more anyway,' says Martha angrily. 'You wouldn't believe how cold it is. I'll just finish the week.' She pulls Sally's coat on. 'I'll miss me mates from work. And the money,' she says bitterly. She notices her friend looking unhappy. 'It's not your fault,

Hilda.' Martha clutches her arm. 'You've been great, really kind. Sally will miss you, and she'll miss Timmy too.'

'I'm sorry . . .' Hilda begins.

'Look, don't worry. I'll find something else, and you're right, Billy can take his turn at minding her. I'll work out something, you'll see. I'll get a job washing up again, or something else.' She laughs. 'At least washing up will keep my hands warm.'

Billy isn't home when Martha returns. He is talking to Frank in a bar.

'Never touch the stuff myself,' says Frank, no surprise showing on his face as Billy produces a joint and waves it under his nose. 'You can keep it,' he says, shifting his weight from one foot to the other and picking up a beer-mat. 'You know very well that in my position it would be curtains professionally if I was caught with it.' He is tapping the beer-mat against the bar. 'You see, it isn't that I have anything against er . . . pot. It's just that it would be a vast embarrassment to be caught with it. In any case there's something I don't like about actually breaking the law, even if one doesn't agree with the law itself.' He pushes the mat away.

'Just thought I might be doin' you a favour.' Billy carefully places the joint in a packet. 'I wasn't trying to flog it to you or anything. Just a little gift.' He smiles.

'Very kind of you. It's the thought that counts.'

'Bollocks,' says Billy.

Frank grins. 'How's Martha and Sally?'

'OK.' He pours most of a pint down his throat. 'Just fine.' He returns the glass to the counter a shade clumsily.

'She tells me she's leaving the job.' Frank turns away towards the barman to order more beer. 'Same again, please.'

'What's that?'

'She tells me she's leaving her job. She told me this evening when I bumped into her on my way back from work. Didn't you know?' says Frank.

'No.'

'Well, well. She says Hilda can't look after Sally any more and that she had an argument with the boss about the cold in the warehouse.' He shakes his head. 'It's too much for her really, looking after everything at home and working all day.'

'No choice,' says Billy. 'What else can we do?'

'Yes, it's very hard, but perhaps you could go back to the building trade.'

'I told you there's nothing around here.'

'So you did.' Frank is demolishing his pint fast. 'Why don't we go down the High Street for the last one?' He nods towards the door. 'I need the fresh air and a change of venue, and it's getting crowded in here.'

'Okay.'

They walk down the High Street. On one corner is a poster that Frank spotted earlier in the evening on his way to meet Billy. It is beside the traffic lights, and he is pleased to see the lights are green, forcing them to hesitate beside the poster before crossing the road. He taps the poster with his umbrella handle. 'There's an idea,' he says, looking at Billy to catch a reaction.

'JOIN THE ARMY AND BE TWICE THE MAN,' says the poster. 'LEARN TRADES USEFUL TO YOU IN CIVILIAN LIFE,' it says below a picture of someone in the foreground leaping over a ditch clutching a machine-gun.

'No good for me,' Billy says. 'Cowards run in my family.'

'You won't see any action.' Frank laughs. 'It's a good life, well paid, and they need bright lads like you.'

'Martha won't like moving away.'

'You get really good accommodation in the army.

131

Married quarters if you have a family. And you can train for any trade, more or less.' Must be careful, he thinks, not to oversell, sound too enthusiastic. 'It's just an idea,' he says, retreating quietly.

'You know I don't want to get married, so I wouldn't be eligible for married quarters. Twice the man,' he murmurs, and laughs. Billy is feigning lack of interest for the sake of being contrary. He'd long contemplated the security and excitement of life in the forces. The Air Force would be his first choice. He fantasized for years about joining the SAS or paratroopers, something which required a bit of bottle, involved fear and drama, to rescue him from everyday drudgery. His work-outs at the gym give him hope that he might make the grade, physically at least. Several times he has written off for the application form but he hasn't filled one in yet. He has a regular little day-dream going for him: episodes enacted in his imagination provide him with a daily fix.

'The lights have changed,' says Frank. 'Come on.'

'Very nice of you to tell Frank you were leaving your job, without consulting me,' Billy says.

'You've been drinking. If you'd been back home earlier I'd have told you about it. Besides, it isn't a matter of choice. You're drunk.'

'I know, get off my back,' he says, turning away. He takes out a joint and lights it. 'They need someone behind the bar in the pub on the High Street.'

'Why don't you take the job?' she says.

'I can't, can I? I need to look for something more permanent and better suited to my nature.' He grins and inhales again, the end of the joint cupped between his hands. 'Besides I have to have some time to enjoy myself. If I was working in a bar I'd never get out in the evenings.' He looks down. 'If you must know, they won't take me, they said they wanted a young woman for the job.'

'Well, you'll have to find something.'

'Don't be so obvious. I thought you could do the bar work when I heard about it and so I told them you'd be in tomorrow. I heard about it soon after Frank told me you'd quit the other place. Sounds like good luck to me, quite a coincidence really.'

'I still don't understand why you didn't try to persuade them to let you do it.'

'I said I need some time to enjoy myself. Don't you understand that? Are you really so incredibly thick?' He crouches on the chair, feet on the seat, knees under his chin, body turned away from her. 'You have to leave me to work out a job in my own time. You know how difficult it is for me to take on all this responsibility, to be tied down. You wanted the baby and I didn't. Now I've done the decent thing and moved in with you and cared for you, don't you think you ought to give a little?' He looks around him. 'Christ,' he says, 'I can't cope with all the harassment.' His head drops down and he hugs his knees. 'You don't understand,' he mumbles. 'If I can't have my freedom at least don't force me to work at some boring job and give up all my time.'

'You know I want you to be happy,' she says. 'But we have to face reality.'

'Reality, reality! You didn't face reality, did you? You knew very well the consequences of having the kid, but would you listen to me? No.' He stands up. 'They won't let me work in the bar, as I've told you, in any case.' He reaches for his coat. 'I have to make a telephone call.'

'Not again, Billy.'

'Now she wants to stop me using the telephone.' He shakes his head. 'I'll see you later!'

She picks up Sally and cuddles her for a while before feeding her and getting into bed herself. She is still awake when he returns. He climbs into bed and turns his back on her. She rolls over and puts her arms around his chest, pulling herself closer to him. No response. She strokes his chest and kisses the back of his neck. No response. She whispers in his ear, 'I love you,' and strokes his face.

'Get off!' He turns on his back. 'Leave me alone.' He reaches across and takes a cigarette from beside the bed.

'Billy, please Billy, don't be like that.' She chokes back tears. 'What's the matter?'

'You can't get enough of it, can you?'

'What's wrong?' She kisses him all over his face.

'Get off.' He sits upright and blows the smoke into the air.

'Billy, Billy, please tell me what's wrong.' She clasps her hands between her knees.

'Every bloody day, you want to make love. Fuck, fuck, fuck. That's all that interests you, isn't it?'

'No, of course not.'

'Ever since you learned how to come you've been the same. I do you a favour and you like it so much you can't leave it alone.' He stubs out the cigarette. 'You don't love me, you just like coming. You just like satisfying yourself.'

'It's not like that. I want to get close to you.'

'Rubbish,' he says.

Next day after work she goes for an interview for the bar job.

'Don't worry about the baby,' she reassures the manager when he hesitates, looking at the child. 'My husband will take care of her.'

'The job's yours, then, love.' He smiles. 'Start next week, OK?'

'Yes. Great,' she says. 'See you then.'

17

SHE NOTICES THE bruise on Sally's cheek when she wipes her face after feeding her. She takes the child to the window and can discern the ghost-like image of four fingers across the side of her cheek. She looks at Billy, who is working-out on his chest expander.

'Did you smack her?'

'When?'

'I don't know.' Martha hitches the child across her body, legs dangling either side of her hip, arm protectively around her.

'She's got a mark on her face, look.' She moves towards him and bends so he can see the bruise. 'Look!'

'Christ. I didn't mean to hurt her. She wouldn't stop crying after you went to work last night.' He brushes his hand across his own face, holding it over his features. 'She wouldn't shut up, wouldn't settle.' He looks down at the floor, tapping his foot. 'It won't happen again.' He bends over and, placing his head on Martha's shoulder, buries his face in her hair. 'I'm sorry.'

'You'll end up hurting her badly if you don't learn to

control your feelings. You've got to stop losing your temper.'

'I said I didn't mean to do it.'

'Make us a cup of tea before I go to work.' She puts the child to bed in the corner of the room while he fills the kettle. 'Did you go to the council offices today?'

'No.'

'If you don't keep at them they'll never get us a flat, even though they promised.' She tucks the covers over the baby and turns around to face him. 'Where did you go then? I told you you had to make a fuss if we're goin' to have any chance of a decent place. I'm pissed off with this room. Besides, if Sally had a room of her own you wouldn't be so bad to her.'

'I'll go down tomorrow.' He pours tea into two mugs. 'Here,' he says, holding one towards her, 'take this,' but he lets it slip before she can grasp it, and it falls to the floor.

'You could have burnt me.' She looks at the mess and wipes splattered tea from her legs.

'I'll see you later,' he says as she puts on her coat ready to go to work. 'I'll come in to see you at work when Sally's asleep.'

'It worries me when you leave her alone.'

'What do you expect me to do? Stay in all night? She's only sleeping, it can't do her any harm. I only come into the bar to see you, don't I?'

'Yes, Billy, but it still worries me. Can't one of your mates babysit while you go out?' Her hand is on the door.

'They've got better things to do with their time. Besides, there's no danger. I only go out when she's asleep, as I have already told you.' He looks agitated, swaying back and forth on his feet. 'No harm will come to her. I can't stay in this place every night while you work. I'll go crazy.' He shakes his head. 'No way will I be stuck, imprisoned, trapped.' He flaps his hands. 'I'll see you later.'

'Billy' – she opens the door – 'you get on down to organize

a flat for us tomorrow, or else.' She hesitates. 'And don't bother coming into the bar tonight, okay?' She slams the door as she leaves.

During the first few weeks of bar work she returns every evening around midnight and slips into bed beside him. He turns his back each time and she lies flat on hers. No words pass between them beyond essential and perfunctory exchanges of information. She thinks that if she shows no signs of wanting to make love, but continues to care for him, it might reassure him that it isn't only his body she wants.

He is making plans. He inquires about joining-up and fills in forms to enrol as a paratrooper. He has one more exciting adventure in store before he will start training to drop from the air, mushroom-shaped silk billowing above him.

'If you keep comin' into the bar while I'm working there's not much point in my goin' to work, is there? You're spending the money I earn faster than I make it,' she says, leaving for work once more.

'Just give me a couple of quid and I'll give it back tomorrow, don't worry.' He stops her at the door, one hand open. 'C'mon girl, give me a break.'

'I'm not giving you any more after this.'

He comes into the bar later. She watches him as he circles the room, changing places each time he orders a drink and observing her as she serves the customers. He leaves just before closing time and someone leaves the bar with him. He does a deal outside and is home before she is.

He is in the bathroom when she climbs into bed. As she pulls the covers open she sees an envelope on her side of the bed. He's not one for writing letters or sending cards, she thinks. And it isn't her birthday for months. She picks

137

up the envelope. Perhaps he's really sorry and can't bring himself to tell her, so that he's written down his feelings, she thinks, and begins to tear it open. There is a five-pound note inside and nothing else. Recognizing its implications she furiously puts it under her pillow. She is not going to give it back to him because she needs the money for food. But she isn't going to make love to him for payment either.

'Did you find the money?' he says, getting in the bed beside her.

'Yes.'

'Well?'

'No, Billy.'

'Not enough?'

'You bastard!'

'Yes, that's right.'

She turns her back and pretends to go to sleep.

Martha looks desolate as she sits on a park bench with Sally in her pushchair. It is late afternoon and the sun glints on the fallen, damp autumn leaves. Frank passes on his way back from school. He notices Martha and Sally and stops the car.

'What's the trouble?' He is getting out of the car.

'Nothing, really.'

'Come on.' He takes her hand. 'I can see you are upset. Come for a walk with Uncle Frank.' He nods towards the child. 'Hello, Sally.' He loops his hand around the top of her arm and guides her as they walk in the park. 'I know something's bothering you,' he says, very quietly, looking into her face. 'You know you can trust me, don't you?' He slides his hand down and slips it around her elbow.

'Everything is going wrong,' she says. 'Nothing seems to work out right however hard I try to sort it out. Billy can't find a job. The work at the bar doesn't pay much, and in fact

I don't think it covers more than the amount Billy spends on booze while I'm working. We can't get a flat and we're still stuck in the same room together.'

'I know, I know,' he says, tapping her hand. 'You have too much responsibility, looking after little Sally, encouraging Billy to get a job, working yourself: there isn't much time left for Martha, is there? No time to enjoy your young life, find out about yourself, have a good time?'

'I never thought about it like that,' she says. 'All I know is I'm exhausted.' They walk a little further. 'However hard I try, nothing improves, and the baby is getting older and needs more space. The situation has deteriorated so much that Billy slapped her the other day.' She looks to Frank for a reaction.

'Terrible.' He shakes his head. 'Terrible. You need someone to give you a break, give *you* something for a change. Someone to care about you. C'mon,' he says, 'come back to my flat and Uncle Frank will make you a nice meal and you can relax for a while and forget about your problems.'

Frank takes the baby and puts her on his lap. 'Sit down, Martha. Put your feet up,' he says, bouncing Sally. 'I'll find something for her to play with while you relax. Look through my records.' He puts the child on the floor and gives her his bunch of keys to chew. 'Find something you like and I'll play it for you.' She notices how delicately he handles the record as he places it on the turntable, lifts the arm, and lets it hover above the spinning disc for a few seconds before releasing it for its slow descent. 'Now' – he turns around – 'what would you like to eat and drink?'

'Anything,' she says.

'I'll see what I can think up, then. While you are waiting I'll show you where the conservatory is and you can relax with my lovely collection of begonias. Sally will love them too. Come on,' he says, and lifts Sally, beckoning Martha to follow him. He tells Sally the different colours, repeating the words, and to Martha he points out the names of each of his precious plants. Then he fetches her a long, cool drink.

There is no more effective trigger than alcohol to start a rage-fired conversation, no better lubricant than kind words and caring gestures to smooth its course. By the time he has cooked and brought her some food, punctuating this process with questions and sympathetic responses, cooing over and soothing Sally, Martha has allowed her problems to tumble out. He smiles and nods. When she hesitates, he prompts her with considered comments, leaning forward to touch her hand. Frank is kind and Frank is good, and he does everything he should.

'Now,' he says as he helps her on with her coat, 'don't forget. You must come here again whenever you feel unhappy. I understand how difficult life can be when things don't work out the way you would like. You're important to me. Remember, I've known you since you were quite a young girl and it matters to me what happens to you.' He puts Sally in her pushchair and fastens the straps to make her secure. They both ease it down the steps, and do not notice Billy in the telephone kiosk opposite.

'Where you been?' He grabs Sally when she hands her to him after arriving home. 'You're late.'

'Never mind.' She watches him place Sally on the bed. 'I just went to the park if you must know.' She watches his face.

'Yes?'

'Yes.' She knows he doesn't believe her. 'I'm late for work. I can't stop to argue.' She turns away.

'Why are you in such a hurry?' He grabs her arm.

'Leave it out.' She pulls away. 'I've no time to talk or I'll be late for work.'

'You're in too much of a hurry.'

'No, I'm not.' She is buttoning her jacket. 'I don't have a choice. God, it's bloody cold out.' She pulls on a scarf which has been hanging across a chair back. 'I'm fed up working all hours, but if I didn't we wouldn't eat, would we, Billy?' Her hand is on the door handle. 'Find something to do yourself, something to bring in the readies, and then I wouldn't have to work so hard. Find something to do!' she snaps.

'I've got something to do tonight,' he says. But she has already banged the door behind her.

18

BILLY PACKS THE ammunition into a couple of the many pockets of his anorak. He rings the bell. Frank opens the door.

'Come in,' he says grinning. 'What a surprise.'

'Yes, I expect it is,' he says, pushing past Frank into the hallway.

'How did you know I live here?' says Frank.

'Martha told me,' Billy lies. 'Thought we might go for a drink or something.' He follows Frank through to the sitting-room.

'Fine. Good idea. I must clear up a few things first, papers, you know. I've an important meeting on school policy coming up soon and I was just sorting through the papers.' He scoops them up. 'Sit down,' he indicates, but Billy is already sitting down. 'What would you like to drink? I'll get you something to keep you happy while I organize a few things.' He holds up a can of beer. 'This be okay?' Billy nods assent. 'Good. You won't mind waiting a while, will you?'

'No.' Billy takes the can and pulls off the tag and drops it

142

on the floor. 'Thanks.' He crosses his legs and takes a swig of beer. 'Get your papers in order,' he says, watching Frank put two files into his briefcase. 'Nice place you got,' he says, looking around the room. 'All right for some.'

'Yes.' Frank zips up the briefcase and gives it a pat. Billy watches him place the case on top of the bookshelf beside the door.

'What's the problem?' Frank eases himself into the armchair opposite Billy.

'Nothing.' He finishes the rest of the beer. 'Why do you ask?'

'Well, you don't usually come here. I mean, you've never visited me here before, so I presume something must be on your mind.'

'No.' Billy folds his arms.

'Sure?'

'I said no. What about another drink, er . . . please.'

'Sure, yes, of course. Another of the same?'

'What choice is there?'

'You can have a whisky if you like.' Frank gets up.

'Thanks.' He watches as Frank pours him a double and nods to indicate water.

'Here.' Frank hands it to him, sits down, and taps the arm of the chair with his fingers. 'What shall we talk about?'

'Anything you like.' Billy turns to look out of the window.

'Er . . . Why don't you relax, take off your jacket?'

'No thanks.' Billy turns abruptly back to face Frank. 'No, I'm cold.' He puts his hands in his pockets.

'You must be nervous. Or sickening for something. It's quite warm in here.'

'I'm fine.' Billy crosses his legs in the opposite direction.

'Why did you never marry Frank? Something wrong with you, is there?' Billy watches as he shifts in his seat.

143

'That's an odd sort of question. Why do you want to know?'

'Well, you are nicely set up here' – he turns both hands towards the room in a sweeping motion – 'and you seem to like children. I don't understand why you haven't married and settled down, as you would say.'

'I cook very well and that saved me from an early marriage.'

'Saved you?' says Billy. 'Er, what do you mean?'

Frank ignores him and continues, 'Well, it's not too late, is it?' He bends over, scratches his ankle, and pulls his sock straight.

'So you can cook, can you? That's nice, because I'm starving.'

'You should have said so before. I'll get you something if you can wait till I see what I have in the fridge.' He goes to the kitchen, relieved to have something practical to do. Billy fumbles with something in his anorak pocket. Frank returns.

'Omelette suit you?' he asks with an obsequious bow.

'Great, thanks.'

'I won't be more than ten minutes preparing it so have another drink if you like and play some music if you're bored' – he nods towards the tape deck – 'while I assemble the food.' He starts to leave but changes his mind and points towards the glass door to the patio. 'If you like plants and flowers I have quite a collection of different species of begonia in there.' He checks to see if Billy is interested, but isn't deterred when he detects no enthusiasm. 'There are some lovely blooms ready now, so have a look at them if you feel like it. I'll just start the food' – and he ducks out of the room again.

Billy looks at his watch, selects a tape, and puts it on the deck. He feels for the small plastic-covered packet of heroin

144

in his pocket. He is reluctant to make too large a capital investment in a venture which will not reap any financial return. So before appearing at Frank's flat he has spent some time chuckling to himself as he cut chalk into the heroin. Initial tests will prove it to be heroin, whether pure or not. But it won't fit the Trades Description Act criteria. What else would you expect a teacher to cut with heroin but chalk, for Christ's sake?

He conceals the packet on a tiny ledge inside a now defunct chimney-breast, and tapes a couple of syringes alongside it. He pours himself a drink and is seated back where he started by the time Frank returns with a tray containing a meal of omelette, sauté potatoes, and salad.

'You should enjoy this.' Frank places the tray on a coffee table.

'Oh, I'll certainly enjoy it.' Billy laughs. 'Aren't you going to eat?

'No, none for me thanks. I've already had something.' He sits down on the arm of the sofa. 'What did you think of the begonias?' Billy nods negatively. 'No. Ah, well, have a look when you've finished.' He collects a drink for himself and suddenly remembers that he has a date with one of his women friends later tonight. He will have to shower and shave and he still has to examine the paper relating to the new decision-making process at the school. By spreading responsibility for decisions he may invite less flak should he realize his ambition of becoming Head Teacher. It is a weighty problem. He recognizes that he volunteered to shoulder more responsibility when he agreed to become Deputy Head, but he has human needs, too, and Sylvia will give him the warmth and comfort he craves. She's not the only one stuck with this burden. There are several other women who have volunteered for this particular role. They are not aware of each other. But he has never made rash

145

promises to anyone and he hopes that he gives as much as he takes. He contemplates the many and exotic delights that lie ahead.

'Very nice.' Billy dumps the plate on to the tray.

'Yes, it is.' Frank shakes his head into gear. He doesn't want to make Billy feel unwelcome too suddenly but he must shove him out of here soon. 'Have a wander around while I rinse these out.' He picks up the tray. 'Don't miss out the begonias, will you?' He points at the patio, feeling slightly silly that he seems to need Billy's approval of his beloved begonias. He disappears into the kitchen.

Can this be true? thinks Billy. Luckily he has something left to plant himself. But not in with the begonias, because Billy recognizes the likelihood of an early, unscheduled discovery by an over-enthusiastic gardener, and that won't do. Another syringe tucked behind the radiator gives Billy a shot in the arm, ha, ha, he thinks as he tapes it securely. Mindful that there should be no give-away finger prints, he wipes everything he touches with a grubby rag from his pocket. He hears Frank whistling and clattering cutlery in the kitchen. Better show interest in the bloomin' begonias. He slips through the patio doors into the tiny roof-top conservatory, and despite himself marvels at the richly coloured plants packed close in earthenware pots, standing in trays of wet gravel on wooden slatted benches around him. He spies the scalpel and meths which Frank uses for leaf and stem cuttings, and wonders whether Frank has a habit or two after all, a secret vice that Billy would never have guessed. He picks up the scalpel and pockets it just in time.

'Pretty good, eh?' Frank stands behind him.

'Yes. Brilliant. I don't know anything about plants, but they seem okay to me.'

'I'm happy to enlighten you.' Frank lovingly bends

towards one of his favourites and touches the pot. 'Ask any question you like.' But he knows it's a lost cause, that there is no way he can transfer any of his interest in them to Billy.

'Do you mind if I have a leak?' Frank nods and follows Billy out of the conservatory. 'Where is it?'

In the bathroom Billy lifts off the cistern lid and thinks what a bleedin' cliché it is to tape another packet of junk to it, but he's exhausted by the tension, it's limiting his imagination and he's cursing the waste. Every pleasure has its price, he comforts himself, as he fits the lid snugly back into place.

'Just what I wanted,' says Frank as Billy emerges from the bathroom. 'Must have a leak myself.' He moves past Billy and shuts the door.

Billy searches his pockets. Yes, one more small deal wrapped in plastic, and Frank's scalpel. He slides silently into the hall, finds Frank's overcoat hanging on a hook, and feels around the inside hem. Good, all stitches in place. He can hear the toilet flush. With the scalpel he cuts the stitching inside the pocket to form a small hole and drops the deal through the hole, into the lining, before swiftly pushing the scalpel back into his own pocket.

He can hear the well-brought-up Frank washing his hands. Finished. Frank opens the door.

'I'm too tired to continue being hospitable this evening, unless you have something important on your mind.' Frank has remembered Sylvia again and the agenda for the meeting. 'I've a lot on at the moment, with an important meeting coming up, as I have already mentioned. School governors, you know.'

'That's okay.'

'Are you sure?'

'I said it's okay.' Billy starts for the front door.

147

'Just a minute, Billy.' Frank is beside him. 'What are you in such a hurry for?'

'No reason.'

'C'mon, mate, I know you. You're looking uneasy. You haven't taken anything, have you?'

'The very idea!' Billy pulls out the insides of his trouser pockets. 'Search me if you don't believe me.' He holds up his arms mockingly. 'Go on.'

'No, no, I didn't mean it. It's just that you have been known to help yourself to things that don't belong to you.' He waves his arms. 'I'm really sorry, old friend. I don't know why I'm so edgy. Really sorry. Come on, I'll stand you one pint around the corner.'

'Trust you,' says Billy, laughing.

'Hello, slag.' Billy is sitting in the dark in their room.

'God, you put the heart across me.' She drops her bag. She's standing at the door after returning from work. 'Why are you sitting in the dark?'

'I've been thinking.'

'Good.' She taps the light on.

'Turn if off.'

'No.'

'I know all about you,' he says.

'Excuse me? What are you talking about?'

'I went to see Frank this evening.'

'Oh.'

'Is that all you have to say?' He spits the words out.

'What do you mean, is that all I have to say? I haven't said anything yet.' She picks up her bag and throws it on the table.

'Well, you better start talking. I won't stand for it. What do you think I am? Comforting yourself, weren't you? Comforting yourself with an old man.'

148

'Oh come on, Billy, he's still in his forties,' she says.

'He's old enough to be your father. Old enough to be mine.' He shouts.

'Is he now? That's interesting. We weren't doing anything wrong.'

'That depends, doesn't it?'

'What do you mean?' She begins to take off her coat.

'What were you doing?'

'We weren't doing anything except talking.' She places her coat across a chair. 'I was fed up. It isn't easy for me, you know, and I had to talk to someone.'

'I'm not good enough for you, I suppose.'

'It's not that. You won't talk to me.'

'I'm talking now.'

'You're shouting.'

'What do you expect?' He gets up.

'We can't go on like this.'

'I've heard that one before somewhere. You know what you are? You're sex-crazy.'

'What are you talking about?'

'You want me to spell it out?' he says.

'Billy, I don't know why you are so angry.' She flops down into a chair. 'I'm just exhausted from work, and I can't face a fight. I'd really like to talk to you, I'd really like to understand you. It makes me sad when you won't listen to me, and treat me like a stranger. Whatever I say you don't seem to want to hear. You don't hear me.'

'I'm shy, I can't explain why. I'd like to be different. I treat everyone the same,' he says.

'Oh great. You treat everyone the same. Everyone you know, or just everyone you're living with?'

'Get off my back.' He bites his lip.

'There you go again. You're cutting me off.' She shuffles the chair closer to him. 'You may not want to hear what I'm

149

going to say and you may not understand what I mean, but I'm going to say it anyway.'

'I hurt,' he says.

'Oh Billy.' She bends towards him, pulls him close, her arms around his neck.

'I want you,' he says.

'No you don't. You just don't want to listen to what I have to say.' She moves away, slips off her shoes, and goes to the basin to take a wash. It has a broken seal around the edge and the smell of rotting wood and accumulated grime isn't pleasant. When she has finished washing she takes a brush and scrubs around the edge of the basin and worries away unresistant débris. She also cleans the small mirror above the sink. She sees Billy's reflection as he gets into bed.

'I could leave tomorrow,' he says as she slips in beside him, 'if you want me to.' He pulls the sheet up over his shoulders as he turns away from her.

'You'll do what you want, whatever I say,' she says.

Early in the morning he is staring down at her as she opens her eyes. He slams down a mug of tea beside the bed. 'There you are.' He slips his hands into his pockets. 'He told me everything, you know.'

'What are you talking about?' She leans on one arm and takes the tea.

'Frank told me everything. I know all your little secrets. He told me it wasn't the first time you'd slept with him. Often paid him visits after school in the afternoons, he said.' He leans over her and pulls the cup from her hand to hurl it across the room. 'Very cosy, you dirty slut.' He coughs, and spits point-blank into her face. As she wipes the spittle away with the sheet, she sees him pick up a holdall, walk to the door, kick it open, and slam it shut as he leaves.

19

DURING THE DAYS following Billy's departure she tries to reorganize her life. She arrives at the bar on the first morning to explain that she cannot work there any more, because she has no one to mind the child and a babysitter would take most of her wages. The manager is annoyed that she has not given any notice, but makes up her wages due and wishes her good luck.

The next day she waits for Frank near the park, on a bench. His car passes but he doesn't appear to see her. The following day she stands near the edge of the pavement and, when he appears, waves her arms to flag him down.

'Get in,' he says. 'But I can't stop, I'm in a hurry.' She puts on the brake of Sally's pushchair and steps into the car.

'Billy has left, gone, vanished,' she says.

'Dear, dear, I'm sorry to hear that, it's very bad,' he says.

'I must talk to you,' she says. 'Billy says you . . .'

'No, not now,' he interrupts. 'It's a bit difficult.' He looks at his watch. 'I have a meeting back at school in half an hour.'

'But you said any time.' She searches his face for some

sign of interest and detects none. 'You said I was important to you, that you care about me. And I want to know what you said to Billy, if you said anything, or if he's inventin' as usual.'

'My dear Martha,' Frank sighs, 'this is a very untimely conversation. I'm busy. I am sure if it is important it can keep for another day. Of course I care about you, but don't misinterpret that.' He leans across her to open the door on her side. 'I don't have time to explain the exact details to you.' He looks at his watch again. 'My meeting is in half an hour and it has long-term implications for the future of the school. So you see it is important to a lot of people . . .' He raises his hands and shrugs his shoulders.

'But you said . . .'

'I'll see you around. Keep well till then.' He turns the ignition, keeping his eyes on her legs.

'Yes,' she says as she slips out of the car and slams the door. 'Yes.'

Frank is preoccupied as he drives home to change and charge himself up for the meeting. He finds his feelings for Martha disturbing and dangerous. He doesn't know if she feels the same way or if he could charm or disarm her. If she shows signs of returning his interest, or needing advice or whatever, he doesn't want to see. He is aware of other teachers who enjoy the pleasures and distractions of relationships with their pupils, and of course at least Martha has left school. But, in addition to the responsibility such an entanglement would entail, there are other ethical considerations. He remembers castigating a friend for playing around with the affections of one of the young women in his class, and at the time he wasn't sure whether he was jealous of his colleague or truly scandalized by his behaviour. And then, of course, there is Billy to consider.

The thought of competing with Billy and losing is more than he can bear to contemplate. If he did find himself involved with Martha, then discovers that she bores him, that he couldn't sustain an interest, that the responsibility is too much, that the disparity in ages bothers him, what then? How could he disentangle himself from someone as vulnerable as she without looking a heel? He only just stops at the red light in time. Gives himself a fright. An irate pedestrian gives him a piece of his mind and taps the bonnet. He must concentrate on his driving.

The meeting ahead is considering a more democratic way of running the school, making decisions by involving parents, teachers, and children. These decisions are becoming more critical now that there is less money to go around. The choices revolve around how to divide the limited funding, where to place priorities, and which resources are to be sacrificed to the efficacy of those activities considered a priority. It isn't looking good for music and art.

It surprises him that some teachers seem to him to reject involvement, say they have enough to do, talk about their salaries and falling standards, and show signs of dis-enchantment. He doesn't like being caught in a situation so complicated and important and where a compromise is inevitable whatever decisions are made. As Deputy Head he doesn't care for the distance that exists between himself and other teachers. This distance will be greater when he reaches the position of Head Teacher, which is on his own personal agenda. He feels lonely.

Two days later Martha has no money left and nothing to eat. When she arrives at the social-security office she has to wait two hours with Sally, who is hungry, before she is interviewed.

153

'When did your husband leave?'

'He's not my husband exactly, but he's the baby's father.'

'Did you live together?'

'Yes.'

'Why did you split up?'

'That's hard to say.'

'Come now, you must have a reason.'

'Of course.'

'Was it sexual incompatibility?'

'What?'

'What was your sex-life like? And would you agree to live with him if he returned?'

'What's that got to do with it? I need money for food.'

'I have to ask you these questions.'

'I don't see what they have to do with having no money.'

'Well, he was the bread-winner, wasn't he?'

'No, I was.'

'Well, then, I don't see what the problem is.'

'I can't go on working and looking after the baby. Besides, when I was working the childminder cost half my wages.'

'I can let you have an emergency payment and if you come back tomorrow I'll see what can be arranged.'

'Mama,' says Sally, 'Mama.' She is restless, tired, and hungry.

Alone for two weeks, she has been to the doctor, who prescribed Valium to 'help her nerves and cheer her up'. She now has a weekly dole cheque for food and rent. Except for her trips to the shops for food with her toddler, she sees no one. She decides to visit the woman downstairs, whom she doesn't know but has seen leaving and entering through the front door. Perhaps if she tries to make friends, she thinks, she will feel less lonely. She rings the bell.

154

'Yes?'

'I'm Martha, your neighbour, I live in the room above, number five.'

'What do you want?'

'Well, I didn't want anything in particular.'

'I'm a very busy person,' says the woman, and shuts the door.

She hasn't spoken to anyone but Sally for several weeks and she doesn't find the Valium takes away enough of the pain of isolation. Whisky, she thinks, will just help her forget, not feel – help her attain a welcome oblivion. But there is no money for such luxuries. She has enough for a bottle of milk. Well, it won't be the first time someone has helped themselves in the local supermarket. She puts on a large old mackintosh that belonged to Billy. She collects the milk from the shelf and places it in the supermarket basket. There is an old wino near the liquor shelf who is clearly intent on exactly the same thing as herself. They have to wait until no one else is watching and then each slips a bottle into a pocket. The wino leers at her. Help, she thinks.

But while she is waiting in the queue at the check-out the remaining few stitches still struggling to hold the pocket together begin to strain under the weight of the bottle and they finally give up the unequal struggle. The broken glass and whisky are spread over so wide an area it is impossible to discern from whose pocket the bottle fell. Like everyone else she walks around the débris as the queue moves forward. The wino winks at her as she leaves after paying for the milk. He nods at her, indicating she come with him, and taps the pocket she knows contains his bottle.

She follows him to the park. They sit on a bench and he extricates a bottle of rum from his inside pocket. She feels mean taking his drink as he shares it with her. She tries to disguise the fact that she wipes the top each time he hands it to her. The sight of his black-hole mouth with one noble tooth standing to attention, the rest gone AWOL, revolts her. He drools, too.

'Don't worry, love, give it a good wipe,' he says. 'Old Jack,' he prods himself urgently and repeatedly in the chest with one grubby finger, 'Old Jack the Lad don't mind.' He gives her a slow-motion wink. 'You and me's alike. What I have I shares.' He gives her a nudge with his elbow. 'What you have I shares, yes?'

'I don't have anything, I'm afraid,' she says.

'Oh yes, you do,' he says, nudging her again, and then takes another slug. He hands her the bottle. She's had enough to live dangerously. She doesn't wipe it this time.

'Thanks,' she says, drinks, and returns it. There is about half left.

'You got somewhere we can go then?' he says.

'No, no.' Through the fuzz she recognizes his intention. 'No, no.' She crosses her arms. Then she remembers Sally alone in her room, waiting for her to return with the milk.

'I've got to go,' she says.

'Hey,' he says as she gets up. 'Don't leave old Jack behind.'

'Look, I've got to go,' she says kindly, turning towards him as he tries to rise from the bench. 'I've got a little girl and I have to feed her.'

'That's just an excuse, love, isn't it?'

'No, really,' she says, 'I can't leave her alone.'

'I revolt you, don't I?' He is stabbing at his chest again with the grubby finger.

'Oh no, it isn't that. It's just that I can't leave my little girl. I expect I'll see you again, Jack' – she waves – 'and thanks for the drink.'

156

'The police are waiting upstairs for you,' says the woman from downstairs.

'What's happening?' says Martha.

'Neglecting your little girl. It's disgusting,' says the woman. 'People like you shouldn't have children,' she sneers.

'What's happening?'

'It's a miracle she's still alive. She was sitting on the window-sill. Three times before I've seen her sitting like that, legs dangling down. She could have fallen any time.'

'Christ,' says Martha, 'why didn't you tell me?'

'I didn't think you minded,' says the woman.

'At what stage would you have told me, eh? Would you have told me if she'd actually fallen and hurt herself? Would you, would you? Silly cow,' says Martha.

'Don't you speak to me like that. They asked me about you. I told them you are always leaving the little mite alone.' She nods her head up and down like a mascot doll in a moving car. 'You're in a lot of trouble, and I can make things worse for you, you know.' But Martha doesn't hear this: she leaps the stairs two at a time, nearly slipping from the effect of the drink.

A policewoman is holding Sally, who puts her arms out when she sees Martha, who takes the child.

'Mama, Mama.'

'Someone has reported that you continually leave your little girl on her own. No, we don't give the name of the people who tell us about child neglect. This is very serious, as she might have come to harm. We are going to take her into care until something better can be sorted out,' says the social worker. 'We'll help you all we can.'

'You can't take her away. I only slipped out to get her some milk.'

'This isn't the first time. It is a serious offence to leave a child under twelve alone,' says the social worker.

157

'But I don't have anyone to leave her with.'

'Then you should have got a babysitter.'

'I don't have any money.'

'Enough to go drinking, apparently,' says the social worker, sniffing Martha's breath. 'It is our responsibility to ensure that children are not put at risk, and your child is at risk. We have had several complaints about her being left alone. If you sit down, we'll have a cup of tea and I'll explain the procedure to you,' she says kindly. 'Can I make some tea?'

'Help yourself,' says Martha, and the social worker moves across the room and puts on the kettle. She returns and sits beside Martha.

'Come on, Martha, it isn't the end of the world. We'll help you settle yourself so that you can keep in contact with her if you sort yourself out, and perhaps you can have her returned to you some day.' She gets up to make the tea, returning with a cup for Martha. As she hands it to her she says, 'I'll take the baby while you drink up.' And Martha hands over Sally. 'These problems take time to sort out, of course. You can ask me any questions you like and I'll explain everything to you.' She goes on to tell Martha that she must return her child benefit book, where Sally will be taken, and that she can visit her child whenever she likes.

'But that's twenty miles away,' says Martha. 'I don't have the bus fare.'

'Well, things have been difficult for you, of course,' says the woman. 'As I've said, we'll do our best for you.'

It is only when they've finished this discussion, and Martha watches them getting in the car with Sally, that the full implication of what is happening hits her. Sally is holding out her arms to her and crying, 'Mama, Mama.'

'Give her back,' Martha screams, as they slam the car door and lock it from the inside. 'Give her back,' she shouts, running after the moving car. 'Give her back,' she shrieks, as she sees Sally's tears pouring down her tiny face, her soft, sweet mouth opening and gulping behind the cold glass of the car window.

'Mama, Mama.'

20

TODAY BILLY WILL make another telephone call. He thinks
he looks good in his uniform; he flexes his muscles before
he puts it on. The daily doses of physical jerks are the
highpoint of each day for him. He will find a telephone box
away from the intrusive eyes and ears of the other young
recruits. The incongruity between the uniform and the
high-pitched voice he has been rehearsing might make
someone curious. He dials the number of the police station
nearest the school and asks for the drug squad. He informs
them that he is a pupil currently at the school where one of
the teachers, Mr Hawkins, has been dealing in all kinds of
drugs, supplying the children at the school. He also tells the
officer that under no circumstances willl he give his name
because he is frightened: the teacher has told the children
he supplies that if they ever grass on him he will ensure
they get bad exam results. By the time he has finished
performing Billy has actually broken into sobs. This elicits
sympathy from the listening squad officer, who promises
confidentiality.

'You've done the right thing in reporting this matter,'
says the officer, 'so don't be frightened to give me your

name. Hello, hello.' But Billy has already replaced the
receiver.

When Frank opens the front door of the flats, he finds two
men standing on the top step. They are as tall as himself.
 'Yes?'
 'Mr Frank Hawkins?' asks one.
 'Yes. Who are you?'
 'We would like to talk to you, Mr Hawkins,' he says,
pulling something from an inside pocket and holding it up
for Frank to see. 'Drug Squad.' He flicks the wallet open.
 'Eh?'
 'Drug Squad, Mr Hawkins. I think you heard the first
time. If we could just step inside . . .' he says. Without
waiting for a response the two men ease their way past
Frank into the hallway. Frank shuts the door and presses
the lift button. They wait in silence, broken only when the
lift door shuts behind them.
 'You want some information?' Frank says. 'I think your
manner is rather aggressive.'
 'Oh yes, we want some information all right, Mr
Hawkins.' The lift stops and they step out.
 'Well, I'm not sure you're going about it in a very
diplomatic way,' says Frank. 'Has there been some trouble
at the school that I don't know about? I know youngsters
often experiment foolishly these days, but I think it's
unlikely at my school. We keep a tight rein.'
 'That may be so . . .' says one of the squad.
 'One of the boys been in trouble?' Frank interrupts.
 'You could say that.'
 'How can I help you? I'd be happy to co-operate in
any way I can, of course, but I think it's extremely unlikely I
can be of any use to you, as I've heard no whispers of any
such problems in my school.' He ushers them through to

161

his living-room. 'Please come this way.' He closes the door.

'Please sit down,' says Frank.

'We prefer to stand, thank you.'

'Please yourselves,' Frank says, sitting on the arm of the chair and crossing his legs. 'You don't mind if I do?'

'It's like this, Mr Hawkins. You are the person who is in trouble.'

'Ha, ha. Very funny.' Frank looks from one to the other. 'This is some kind of jape, yes?' No response still. 'I see not.' He sits down into the seat of the armchair. 'I suggest you explain yourselves.'

'You won't object if we examine your flat, will you?' says one of the men.

'Er, no of course not, always pleased to oblige the law, though I cannot see to what purpose. You won't find anything of interest to you.' He remembers the stack of nudie magazines he has put in the third drawer down in his desk. 'I think I have some rights in this matter. There is the small question of a search warrant.' He can see the newspaper headlines about 'Deputy Head of school in vice squad round-up'. But of course that would be ridiculous in this day and age. He is not looking forward to them finding the mags, but perhaps they can all share a laugh and leer. 'Search warrants, please,' he says.

'As drug squad officers we do not require such documents.'

'Ah, I see. However, this seems to me an intrusion of my privacy, and I suggest to you that you should at least have substantial evidence of something, which is impossible in this case, before making such an invasion of my property. Don't let me influence you, of course, don't let my position intimidate you, you must do what you want. I'm trying to save you from looking foolish, and I shall expect an apology.' Frank stands up.

162

'I assure you we have the evidence required and have no intention of wasting any more time,' he barks at Frank. 'My colleague and I will proceed to search the premises.'

'Go ahead. But as I said, I shall expect an apology.'

'A very nice performance, Mr Hawkins,' one of the squad officers says as he watches Frank's horrified expression as each new hiding-place reveals another stash of junk, or syringes. 'Very nice performance.' He turns to his companion. 'Wouldn't you say it is worthy of an Oscar?' His comrade nods, and he turns to Frank again. 'You should audition for Margate Repertory Company, if and when you ever get out.' He hands the latest find to his colleague, who places it in a plastic bag with the rest of the haul. 'You'll find they have a very good amateur theatre group in the local nick. I suggest you use your evident theatrical talent to good use. Very gifted performer, I must say.'

'I can't think how this stuff got here in my flat. There's been a ghastly mistake. Somebody's planted it on me. Oh my God, you can't believe I use the stuff. Take a blood-test' – he holds out his arm – 'you'll see for yourself.'

'Nice one, Mr Hawkins. It's worse than that. Dealing is a far worse crime than simple use. And supplying juveniles is treated very gravely by the local beaks. I assure you that any teacher who abuses his position by corrupting the children in his care is dealt with very severely indeed. In fact' – he slips the plastic bag into his case – 'in fact, although it is not my position to make any comment, simply to collect evidence, I think' – he draws himself up and leans close to Frank's face – 'you're just about the lowest form of life, next to child molesters and murderers.' He leans back, swinging on his feet. 'You'd better get in the car and we'll take you down to the station immediately. No trouble now!'

'But I haven't done anything.'

'Tell that to the judge.'

Black plastic covers the thin mattress on a slatted wooden bench along one wall of the cell in the police station. Frank notices the blankets piled unevenly on to it. The detective is beckoning towards Frank.

'Take off your tie, belt, jock-strap, and shoes.'

'Why?'

'Work it out for yourself. Just take 'em off.' The detective holds out one hand. Frank undoes his laces and slips his feet from the shoes and hands them over.

'I see you have no belt, but what about a jock-strap?'

'What do you want to know for?' Frank pulls his jacket closed and folds his arms.

'Take a guess. I can always strip-search you if you want to make things difficult for yourself. Or perhaps you'd enjoy that, eh?'

'I want to speak to my solicitor.' Frank undoes his tie and holds it in both hands as if there might be an exchange. 'I have a right to legal advice.'

'Drop your pants.' Frank stuffs the tie in his pocket and pulls down his trousers; the detective checks to see he isn't wearing a strap. 'Okay, pull 'em up.'

'Now can I see my solicitor?'

'On our terms, mate, not yours. You have a right when we decide you have. Got it, Mr Hawkins?' The detective grabs the tie. 'If we think it may interfere with our investigations we can delay your consultation with the solicitor until we are satisfied it will not.'

'But I have a right to make a phone call.'

'You made one.'

'There was no reply.'

'But you made one.' He turns and slams the cell door shut.

'How long are you going to keep me in here?' Frank grabs the bars like he's seen them do in the movies.

'Sleep tight,' says the detective as he turns the key in the lock.

'Shut up,' comes a voice from under the blankets on the bench. 'Can't a bugger get a decent night's kip?' The blankets heave as a body turns over. Frank has company.

The company doesn't have very refined manners. Turning the body has disturbed the already churning contents of his stomach and before he has entirely removed the blankets covering his face he heaves himself over the side of the bench and a sandwich-spread-coloured mess is disgorged from his mouth and splatters onto the floor. 'Now I feel better I think I'll have a wank.' The company's hand moves to his trouser zip as he looks up at Frank. There is a string of puke adhering to his chin. He grins at Frank. 'Help yourself.' He gestures towards the floor. 'Get yourself a spoon, mate, and you can have it for breakfast.' He laughs, seeing the expression on Frank's face. 'Egg, I think it was.' He looks down at the mess. The door opens and Detective Sleep-tight calls Frank.

'Come on, Mr Hawkins, we're ready to interview you now.' He locks the door behind Frank and they walk the long corridor in silence and enter the interviewing-room.

'Sit over there,' says the detective indicating a wooden chair. Frank sits down. 'We'll wait for my colleague before we begin. Are you sitting comfortably?' The door opens and the other detective carries in a plastic cup filled with coffee, which he offers to Frank.

'Do you take sugar?' he asks.

'No.'

'Good.' He hands the cup to Frank. 'Much better for the health. Just drink that up and take your time about it. I can understand if you feel a bit shocked, it's a very nasty business for you.'

21

BILLY HAS FINISHED the day's work-out and is reading a newspaper on his bunk this evening, having declined his mate's invitation to play darts and have a pint. The front page is filled with talk of war. It won't come to anything, of course. No, Britain wouldn't be so foolish as to involve itself in armed conflict; it's all sabre-rattling. That's the lads' opinion. The barracks is buzzing with speculation. The officers won't discuss the subject with the ranks. They are not usually so taciturn or reluctant to voice opinions; perhaps they actually know something!

On page five Billy finds what he is looking for. 'School-teacher in Vice Ring.' 'Teacher Frank Hawkins, Deputy Head of the local comprehensive school, was arrested yesterday on a drugs charge and is still being questioned. The police are looking for a young man, a contact of the teacher, who may be implicated in the crime, says a police spokesman.'

Billy screws up the paper and lobs it into the bin. He thinks, if I had been found with all that incriminating stuff in my room they wouldn't be looking for anyone else. Frank must have fingered him. Bloody grass. At least he doesn't know where Billy is. No one can trace him without releasing his name to the press and, even then, there is more than one Billy Watts in this world; besides, he has enlisted under his full name of Michael William Watts. They can search for him through Job Centres or whatever but they won't trace him for a long time if he stays in the armed forces. Until he can find some way out of the situation, or some alibi, Her Majesty's Forces is a safe place for Billy.

After twenty-four hours in the police cell, Frank is permitted a visit from his solicitor, John, an old friend whose professional services he hasn't required since the conveyancing of his flat.

'Forgive me, Frank, but I have to formally ask you, are you guilty?'

'No. Of course not.'

'Okay, okay, it's just a formality, as I said.' John's glance slides away from Frank's face. 'It's a tricky situation because there is so much circumstantial evidence, and in the case of drugs, well . . . it is very incriminating, and frankly' – a little laugh – 'frankly, I don't remember anyone getting off such a charge. Of course possession doesn't necessarily imply that you've been dealing, they would need more evidence than I think they have. Or than I know they have, anyway. But possession, well, that's the problem.'

'I was er . . . framed.'

'Any idea who would want to frame you, and why?' He looks at Frank as if he had fallen out of a tree. 'What sort of company have you been keeping?'

'I'm sure it is an ex-pupil of mine, Billy Watts. He's always been troublesome, and he disappeared shortly after visiting my flat, several months ago. I tried to befriend him.'

'Did he try to blackmail you?' John's eyebrows rise.

'No, you misunderstand me, it wasn't anything like that. I felt sorry for him. He's the only person I know who could obtain the stuff, and also have the imagination and basic meanness to set me up.'

'But why should he do it?'

'Absolutely no reason I can think of.'

'Are you sure it isn't one of your lady friends getting some kind of revenge after you've given her the brush-off?'

'No, definitely not, it's nothing like that. Suppose we can trace Billy Watts? I suppose it will depend on his confession whether I'm found guilty or not.'

'More complicated than that, I'm afraid. They'd drop the charges, of course, if he admitted framing you.'

'I want to stand trial. I want to be found not guilty. I want *him* in the dock.'

'Hold on, old man. Even if this gets to court and you are found not guilty, the mud will still stick. That's what is bothering you, isn't it? You want to clear your name?'

'Of course. How would you feel in my position? I'd really like to sue the police for wrongful arrest.'

'I'm not sure I would advise you to do that. We'll see what happens. Now, I'll take down any details you can remember and then advise you what your next step should be.' He takes out a pen.

Next day, Frank is released on his own bail. He walks out into a clear evening and decides to take a walk. He cannot confront the loneliness of his own flat nor the camaraderie of the pub and the inevitable questions. He is aware that the school has been informed of his arrest and the papers have been running the story. It is a long walk; he alternates between being angry and feeling guilty. He feels dirty, yes,

168

grubby. Why? He needs to work this out before facing anyone. He doesn't trust himself to keep his dignity. Will he break down? He must walk until he has resolved what to do. He wonders how Martha has coped since he last saw her, after Billy left. At least he has some money. He can consider a new start, move away, find a different job. Or can he? He is nervous of moving away from the flimsy security he has built up for himself. He imagines facing the school governors; they are notorious for being divided on every issue, a result of democracy in action, he thinks. The irony of his own part in encouraging this level of democracy is not lost on him.

He doesn't relish their response to his arrest. They will have to put the interests of the school first. There will be no doubt about where their priorities will lie. Any chance of becoming Head Teacher is gone forever. Now it is likely he'll be asked to resign in the interests of the school's reputation. There is no escape. He steps into a dark doorway to blow his nose and wipe away the tears that threaten to fall.

He continues walking, his concentration detaching him from the noise and activity of the streets around him, until he is disturbed by a police siren and a flashing blue light. He is rooted like Lot's wife, transformed into salt because she turned back to face the decadence she was fleeing; the image puzzles him but there is no time to speculate on the significance of this as the car screeches to a halt. God, what are they coming to get him for now?

They slam the squad car doors, walk past him towards a crowd. A woman is shouting, surrounded by the silent crowd; she is the cabaret act for the night, but they do not applaud. She begins to sing an old music-hall song as the officers approach. They are on either side of her, attempting to persuade her to come with them. She sits down. They are rougher now, trapping her arms behind her back, pulling her upright and forcing the top half of her body forwards.

Frank, white with rage, adrenaline pumping through his body, thinks fast: could he claim she is his wife? Mother? But he cannot guess her age, and in any case the incongruity between her clothes and his suit would make this implausible. He steps forward and, pulling himself up to his full height and with a quiet hope that they aren't the cops from the station, says:

'Excuse me, officer.' His voice is imperious and calm. 'I'm her doctor. I've been looking for her all evening.' He coughs, giving time for thought. 'She is in need of urgent medical attention.'

'Good evening, Sir, er . . . doctor,' says the officer nearest to him. 'She's been causing a disturbance. We've had two complaints from local residents about her shouting and singing.'

'Well, she's my patient and I'll take charge of her.' He takes her arm. 'Don't you chaps know when someone is ill? It should be part of your training. You could do her a lot of harm if you locked her up. I'll take her back to the hospital and she'll trouble you no further.' The woman nods wildly.

'Yes, of course.' The policeman is looking confused, and turns about him to see what his colleague makes of it.

'Take your squad car off and do something more useful with it.' Frank looks at the crowd. 'Had your fun then? Go and find something else to amuse you instead of jeering at this unfortunate woman,' he shouts, spit spraying. He steers her away. 'Come on,' he whispers, 'let's get out of here fast before they start thinking.' He holds her arm as they set off.

The officer is running after him. 'Would you like a lift to the hospital?'

170

'No thanks.' Frank winks at him, and nods towards the woman. 'We're just going to have a cup of coffee to calm ourselves down before we go back to the hospital. I have a car around the corner. But thanks.'

A few streets away they find a café.

'Listen, you bugger, you lost me my bed for the night,' she says.

'You mean you want to be locked up?' Frank leans across the table.

'Well, of course I don't, but in this cold weather a body needs a bit of home comfort, like the local nick. I've nowhere to go, see.' She blows on her hands before warming them around the cup of coffee. 'Ah, here it comes.' She moves the cup to make way for a plate of food. 'Thanks for this.' She smiles up at him. 'I can get a place in a night shelter sometimes, if there is room. And I like to move about, you see.' She begins to eat. 'This is very nice. What possessed you to come to my rescue? Quite the white knight in shining armour, eh? It's never happened to me before, kind sir! I hope you are not looking for any favours from me.' She looks down. 'I'm not like that, you see.' She is silent for a minute.

'Of course not.' Frank suddenly realizes what she means. 'No, no, just eat up, and enjoy your food. I feel very silly about unintentionally scuppering your plans, so to speak.'

'The food will keep me warm tonight, as I shall now have to sleep in the railway station, which gets very chilly in the early hours of the morning.'

'You could spend the night at my place. At least I can compensate you that way for my stupidity.'

'You mustn't worry about that. It's the thought that counts, isn't it, as they always say.' She laughs. 'I think it was very amusing. They were completely taken in by you. I couldn't think what you were up to when you interfered,

171

but I've always been one for a bit of an adventure myself.'

'Would you like something to drink?' Frank turns around to see if they serve alcohol.

She shakes her head. 'Never touch the stuff.' She looks up to watch his face for a reaction. 'Are you sure you wouldn't mind me staying at your place? You may have noticed I am not too clean – because I haven't had a bath for weeks. Too cold, you see.'

'I shouldn't worry about that,' he says. 'I could do with the company anyway, so you'd be doing me a favour.' He laughs. 'You can tell me all about your adventures.'

At the barracks, Billy is working-out in the gym. He is wearing a singlet, shorts, and boxing gloves, pummelling a punch-bag, and thinking about the headlines in this morning's paper. He never thought it would come to this: when he joined up no one had suggested he'd ever see serious action. He had watched a squad leave for Ulster just after he had enlisted, and that had made him a bit nervous. Now there was talk of troops being sent to defend some island thousands of miles away. Punch, punch, he smacks the bag hard. He doesn't want to be shot, burnt, or blown to bits. He is frightened of the pain. Slap, slap goes the punch-bag; it grazes his chin as he ducks too slowly when it returns.

There is another thought pushing aside the anxiety about armed combat, struggling to be resolved; it concerns Frank Hawkins. A paragraph in the paper revealed that he'd been released on bail, with the probability of charges being dropped when the man the police would like to question is found. They are stepping up their inquiries. But they must never find Billy: then the charges against Frank will never be dropped. He takes off the boxing gloves and hurls them away.

If he goes AWOL to avoid being sent to fight, he will get picked up. What chance will he have with both military and civilian police stalking him? None. He chalks his hands and walks to the parallel bars.

Sure, if he goes to the war-zone he will get killed. He has only to consider his own history of failure to know that. He has failed at everything except physical training. He leaps onto the bar and swings his legs. He has failed at being a kid, a lover, a father, and now he has even failed at revenge.

He bruises his thighs against the bar as he takes the somersault too fast and clumsily. He would like to fill Frank Hawkins' fucking mouth with pebbles and punch him in the gob. Tee-hee-hee. That would take the bleedin' ho-ho smile off his face. He is over the bar again. There is one way out of this stinkin' mess, he thinks. He still has contacts that can fix things. He lands perfectly balanced, both feet together and no hesitant step forward.

22

SHE SEES THE tiny baby on the ground, its head broken on one side, the brains pouring out on to the floor, glistening in the half-light. How can she help it? It is no good scooping up the slimy matter and putting it back inside. It is opening its mouth and crying silently. She wants to cradle it in her arms and make it better but she knows you can't fix a shattered, smashed head. What has she forgotten, what was it that Billy told her to do?

She wakes sweating, her pillow damp from her tears, and remembers her mute, sterile screaming. She closes her eyes and again the dream returns. Is it some morbid curiosity which draws her to dwell on the images of her dream, so easily conjured up when she closes her eyes? Or is it familiarizing herself with something inevitable, rehearsing for the worst?

She shudders as she shakes herself fully awake, squats on the bed, and stares unseeing for a long time in the direction of the window in her room, incapable of, and uninterested in, discerning the time of day. She hasn't eaten for three days. What has she forgotten? What was it that Billy told her to do? Billy. Billy. Where has he gone? Where is anyone? Most of all, where is Sally?

Her limbs are stiff and awkward as she unfurls herself and rises. She stands at the window and, with as much resolve and strength as she can muster, slams her fist into the glass. Her intention is to smash it and crash her wrists down on to the broken edge, but the bloody window doesn't break.

There is a plastic bag containing ancient refuse beside the sink, which advertises itself in no uncertain way. The stench of its wretched decaying matter churns what little remains in her stomach. She will empty the bag and squat curled up inside. She will wait until the absence of sound tells her that the household is asleep, wait until the noise of cars outside is reduced to a level which indicates that only the furtive early-morning revellers are returning to their patches and will not notice her, and, in the gap between them and the roundsmen and early shift workers, she will take the empty bag downstairs. She will sit inside it, the open end tucked and tied under her feet, and wait until she suffocates. In the morning, when the refuse lorry comes, they will pick her up with all the other rubbish and place it in the crusher.

Someone is banging on the door. She ignores the sound and listens motionless as footsteps die away.

She fumbles around in the dark for the bag, bumping her elbow on the sink as she searches for it. No fucking money for the meter so no light. She pushes the bag on to its side and pulls the bottom corners, emptying the contents onto the floor. Christ, no, the stink would knock a dog over, now it's fully exposed. She'd throw up if she could; the saliva in her mouth is threatening action.

The Valium will help your nerves, the doctor had said. Too true, she thinks. The more the better. If one will ease

175

the situation, soften the blow, push away the pain of separation from Sally, take away the feeling of desolation and replace it with no feeling at all, think what a whole bottle could do. It might do the job permanently.

Fumbling around again in the dark her fingers touch but do not fully grasp the bottle of Valium. She dislodges it from the shelf; it falls to the ground and just catches the sharp nail-top sticking out from a loose floorboard. Down on the ground she flattens her hand and picks out the pills from the glass. Curses, glass only breaks when you don't want it to. When she has recovered a handful of happiness pills she fetches a glass of water. Nice one, NHS. Pity they can't supply food and light too. But at least they provide the final solution free, when there's nothing else left. She gulps down three at a time, with water, until she has devoured the lot.

Soft, sunny, early-morning beach crunching under bare toes, sand-full mouth. She sees sun-light, hears the shrill cry of happy children. But there is something nasty behind the stone. Leg slowly contracting. She feels it soft and warm in her throat. Bring it up. Spit it out. There is something sharp pecking at the inside of her lips. She must open her mouth, let it out. Open wide, a bird flies out. Banging noise and siren sounding.

Somewhere over the Southern Hemisphere a Hercules aircraft filled with Our Boys takes them towards the action. Billy has strapped a filled syringe to his arm, the needle inserted into the vein and taped securely. He has used a scalpel to cut the arm seams of his uniform and flak jacket and then tacked them together in order that he can easily pull the seams apart to get at the plunger on the syringe when he wants to. The door of the Hercules is open. He will be the tenth man to jump.

'Mugs! No, green bottles!' he says under his breath while waiting in the queue. He laughs softly to himself when he considers he's going to do his bit of killing in the name of Queen and country. 'Fall guys,' he chuckles and is nudged towards the exit.

'Jump!' says the officer.

'No, jerk off,' says Billy. 'It's time for the big ejaculation.'

He takes off spreadeagled. He can push the plunger on the syringe and then pull the rip-cord. But if he pushes the plunger he won't need to pull the rip-cord. He pushes. He holds out his arms.

'Pull the cord,' shouts the first man out as he sees Billy plummet past him. 'Pull the cord,' he screams. He isn't sure, but he thinks he hears Billy shout:

'I'm flying.'

In the casualty ward they never turn the light off. All night long. They tell Martha they have washed her insides out. But they didn't get THEM out. She is moved to a psychiatric ward.

They've broken through, under her skin, nuzzling and burrowing their way to get at the juiciest, tastiest bits of her entrails. She can feel them gnawing at her guts. If they tried to remove them how would they know the difference between them and her intestines: they look much the same, don't they? She claws at her side, trying to pull at them. 'Get them out.'

'I can't see anything.' The doctor examines her body, expert fingers pushing gently down on the area around her peritoneum. 'There's nothing wrong with you.' He pulls the covers up and she tears at her side again.

'Liar,' she shouts.

She knows they are sucking at her slimy visceral matter, greedily gulping down bits of her. If she doesn't get them out they will devour her completely and she won't exist any more.

'Get them out, get them out.' She twists and turns.

'There's no one here except you and me and the nurse,' he says.

'You're blind,' she says.

'I'll give you something to help you relax.' He squirts a little of the contents of the needle into the air before handing it to the nurse. 'I'll see you in the morning.' He is gone.

Ga-ga pills each morning, noon and night. She won't move. Try to stand up today, they say. But she cannot. She won't eat unless they feed her. She lets it dribble out of her mouth so they have to scoop it up and push it in with a spoon. She lies curled up, always clawing at the same side. Sometimes when they sit her up to feed or wash her she flaps her arms in the air.

This morning she wakes and finds the doctor staring down at her. 'How are we today?' He is holding her hospital record sheet. Can't he see them squirming around, getting fatter? With the nurse's help he pulls her into a sitting position. 'Let's have a look at you.' He tries to pull her stiff arms away from her side, unsuccessfully. But he still doesn't see them. 'I've never seen anyone behave like this before.' He sits on the bed and examines her record thoughtfully for a few minutes.

'I see you have a little daughter. I'm sure she's missing you.' Martha pulls the sheet over her head. 'I know you must want to see her again and look after her yourself and there is no reason why you shouldn't if you get better.' He taps the clipboard with his pen. 'There's no reason you won't get better, is there? No. We want you to tell us what is wrong because we don't understand unless you explain it to us. Come on, Martha, tell me what's wrong, tell me what's eating you?'

178

'Maggots,' she says.

He turns away. 'Maggots to you, too,' he whispers, and after folding his stethoscope tucks it in his pocket.

Someone is cracking the top off a phial just outside her open door. She can imagine the needle being inserted and the cocktail withdrawn into the syringe. I'm glad they're not doing it outside the victim's door, she thinks, feeling waves of sympathy for the recipient. At least they have the sensitivity to avoid the patient hearing the preparations. The nurse doesn't know why she laughs when the door opens further and she strides towards her holding the syringe, and it dawns on Martha that the injection is for her rear.

During one of those hardly-awake moments before sleep intervenes and when daydreams receive their most fanciful embellishments – the effect of which is heightened by the liquid cosh administered at regular intervals – Martha can feel someone pushing back the hair from her forehead and gently slipping a hand around her head. She blinks her way awake. At first she thinks a large, old, pink tortoise is staring, face close to hers, hooded eyes flickering in their sockets, tough and wrinkled. Wispy grey hair, caught for a moment by the breeze from the open window, is still again. Eyes that have seen eternity settle on hers.

'I want to play with you.'

'Thththughgh.' Martha tries a word but it is trapped in a bubble on the end of her tongue as she tries to force it through her mouth.

'I'm Edie.' Her hand is tapping Martha's. 'You're called Martha, aren't you?' She points to the chart at the end of the bed. 'I can read now, you know.' She claps her hands. 'Clever me. I've been watching you and you don't have anyone to play with, do you?' Martha nods. 'I didn't think

179

so. I'll be your friend if you like,' she says with satisfaction, taking Martha's hand in hers. 'I'll show you my secret some time.' She claps her hands together again. 'And I'll let you come to my ninth birthday party.'

'Stop talking daft, Edie,' the nurse says not unkindly. Edie looks fierce; a challenge hangs in the air. 'Now, you naughty girl, you know you're not nine any more,' she says as she takes Edie's arm and helps her to stand upright, stiff old bones jamming in awkward positions. 'Come on, it's time for your dinner. It'll get cold if you don't hurry.'

'I'll see you after I've had my dinner,' says Edie, and Martha watches her shuffling away, odd slippers flapping at her departing heels, body leaning to starboard against the nurse, head bent in concentration. She stops with the effort after a few paces, gaining breath for the final straight, pats the nurse's hand tucked in her arm. 'We're good girls,' she says before forcing herself forward again.

Each day Edie visits Martha, sometimes helping to feed her, and after lights-out at night she sits on her bed and tells her stories. One night she slips slowly into bed beside Martha and says:

'I'll let you feel my secret.'

'You better not get too near me,' Martha mumbles. 'You might catch the maggots, they might gobble you up too.'

'I'm not frightened of a few silly old maggots.' Edie makes herself comfortable. 'They don't bother me.'

'Have you seen them? Everyone else pretends they're not there.'

'Of course I have. But I have Holy God to protect me, watch over me.'

'I wish he'd watch out for me.'

'Watch over, not watch out for.' Edie moves closer to Martha.

'Watch over,' says Martha.

'And God is she, not he.'

'She,' says Martha.

'Here,' – she pulls something from her pocket – 'feel this.' Martha can feel something tubular in Edie's hand. 'In the morning, when the world has turned upside-down again and it's dark on the other side, I'll show you how it works.'

Nudge, nudge, goes Edie in the dawn light. Martha, numbed by knock-out pills, is slow to respond. 'Come on,' says Edie. 'Time to get up to see the secret. We can share it.' She looks coyly at Martha.

'Share it,' says Martha.

'You're my best friend,' says Edie.

'Best friend.'

They dodge their way past the night staff, up an empty corridor, until they reach an alcove at the furthest corner, around a bend, away from prying eyes. There is an east-facing window set in the alcove. Edie takes the kaleidoscope from her dressing-gown pocket and hands it to Martha.

'If you shake it and look again it will be different. Every time you move, turn or shake it, it forever changes. Hold it up to the light and look through that little hole there.' She claps her hands and, clinging to Martha's arm, tries little stumbling jumps.

'I can see a star, I can see butterflies.' Martha is jubilant.

'You'll see anything you like if you look long enough,' she whispers.

Martha, mesmerized by shards of sapphire, relishes slithers of silver, sees scarlet on fire, golden saffron dance before her, while emerald glitters and winks, wild onyx throws shadows, bright stipples of violet, lapis streaks, luscious crimson and ice glisten and sparkle, singing before her delighted eye, rose-tinted as dawn sprinkles the day with life.